SAM CRESCENT & STACEY ESPINO

**EVERNIGHT PUBLISHING ®**

www.evernightpublishing.com

Copyright© 2018

**Sam Crescent and Stacey Espino**

Editor: Karyn White

Cover Artist: Jay Aheer

ISBN: 978-1-77339-721-4

**SAM CRESCENT & STACEY ESPINO**

# CLAIMING HIS PRIZE

## *Killer of Kings, 5*

### Sam Crescent and Stacey Espino

### Copyright © 2018

### Chapter One

Chains was hungry.

No, starving.

He needed food.

After all the shit that went down with Shadow and Boss at Killer of Kings, he'd decided to take a vacation. He didn't want, nor did he need, any shit in his life right now. At times, being a killer took a toll on a man, and he wasn't a fool. His kill ratio rivaled many of the killers he associated with. Of course, Boss had overtaken all of them with the slaughter he'd just done based on a mafia mark.

Rubbing the back of his shaved head, Chains entered a shitty looking diner. He'd have preferred a restaurant, one that served Russian food, but right now he couldn't be picky. Taking a seat in the back of the diner, he grabbed the well-worn menu and looked over the choices. Of course, it was all greasy burgers and stuff more suited to a fifties-style menu.

His cell phone buzzed, and he glanced down to see it was Boss.

The fucker was alive and well, not that he would

ever doubt him. If anyone could get out of a hit, it would be Boss.

Turning off his cell phone, he placed it back in his pocket. He'd already left word for Boss to know he intended to have some time off. No killing.

To get this … burning under control.

The rage inside him had begun to simmer midway through this latest mission, watching Shadow with Riley. He didn't know what it was all about, and he didn't care either. All he knew was when he wanted to kill those he worked with, he had to leave.

So far, Viper, Bain, Killian, and now Shadow had each fallen for a woman. Hardened killers became weak when they chose to bring a woman into their lives. Killers shouldn't have women. They always had a "use by" date, and if one of their enemies heard of a way to take them out, their women would be the first to go. It was why he never allowed himself to take any pleasure other than in the women he paid for. The whores on the streets wanted his money, and he only required a quick release.

If he didn't feel like fucking one of the streetwalkers, he'd found plenty of escorts and agencies willing to give him what he wanted.

He didn't want love.

Glancing around the diner, he saw several families eating. One of them had that very prim and proper American look with crisp white shirts, the kind they wore to church.

He stared at them, knowing how looks could be deceiving. In his line of work, he'd seen a lot of shit. He'd seen stuff that had sickened him to the core.

One of the worst things was the child trafficking rings. Boys and girls sold for a fortune to meet the demands of the depraved perverts that wanted them.

After seeing some of the victims, he'd made a vow to always defend them. If he ever caught sight of anything going down, he checked it out, and was sure to make an example of the people who thought they could use vulnerable children.

After surviving one of the worst childhoods imaginable, Chains learned from a young age the horrors that awaited in the big wild world. He'd been an unlucky bastard, being thrust into one of the worst Russian orphanages.

Every one of them had to learn to survive, and that hadn't been the worst of it. The people who claimed to protect them had enabled the abuse. He'd been in a mixed gender orphanage, and the girls that were there, they had it a lot worse than the boys. They were trained to shut up and take it.

As a child, seeing the damage those girls faced at the hands of men, he'd taken a personal dislike to anyone who harmed a child.

"Hey, sorry it took me so long. What can I get you?"

The feminine voice brought his attention around to the woman standing in front of him. He'd seen her enter five minutes ago. Her head was bent over her notepad, and she was on the chubby side. The uniform she wore was too tight, some of the buttons gaping around her impressive cleavage.

Her long brown hair was pulled back into a ponytail, and she looked pale. He couldn't get a good look at her, and Chains wanted to look at her.

"What's good here?"

He'd long ago lost any of his Russian accent, and only when he was angry did it show. Right now, he looked and sounded like any American businessman. He always preferred suits. To him they'd symbolized the sign of power, where the real money was.

"The cheeseburger's good. I, erm, I wouldn't go for the chicken though."

"Oh, why not?"

The girl, Lori, her badge said, looked behind her, and he saw her nerves show through. "He doesn't always cook it all the way, and it can make you sick."

She still hadn't looked up, and he didn't like that she was avoiding eye contact.

Putting his hand at his side where his gun rested, he wondered if any of his enemies had followed him. He could never be too cautious in his line of work.

Lori sniffled and leaned to the side, expelling a little cough. She sounded sick.

"I'm so sorry." She cleared her throat, and she finally looked up at him.

The bruise covering her left eye twisted his gut.

His gaze unnerved her as she quickly arranged the hair covering her eye. "What can I get you?"

The bruise looked recent. "You know, boyfriends that do that don't deserve you, right?"

"What?" she asked.

He pointed to his eye as he looked at her. "The eye. You really shouldn't stick around with a guy like that."

Her cheeks heated, and she shook her head. "Oh, this isn't from a boyfriend."

Okay, now he didn't like where this was going.

"I was just in the wrong place at the wrong time. So, cheeseburger, right?"

Chains watched as she quickly wrote down the order. He wasn't about to dispute her.

"What's your last name?" he asked.

"Why?"

"Because I'm a curious customer."

She took a deep breath, and shrugged. "Dean. Lori Dean." She walked away, and he watched her go before grabbing his cell phone.

Turning it back on, he put a call in to Maurice. He didn't like that she didn't put up enough of a fight. Didn't she have a clue what a guy could do with her name, and only her name?

"What do you want?" Maurice asked.

"Is that any way to greet me?"

"Boss doesn't have any jobs right now, and it seems his employees like to use my services for their personal benefit."

"You make a lot of money from it," Chains said, reminding him of the extortionate fee he charged. He knew for a fact Maurice didn't charge Boss half as much.

"A guy's got to make a living somehow."

He rolled his eyes. "I want you to find out everything you can about a Lori Dean. Looks young, twentyish." He told him the name of the diner where she worked.

"Fine."

Maurice hung up without even saying goodbye. Pocketing his cell phone, Chains watched Lori as she moved from table to table. Her wide hips had a natural sway, mesmerizing him.

She came back with a large pot of coffee. "Coffee?" she asked.

"Who gave you the shiner?"

Lori poured him some coffee and tutted. "You know that's rude to ask a lady."

"Yeah, well I think it's rude for a guy to hit a woman." He saw her tense up, and he hated that he made her nervous. It wasn't his intention.

She kept a good distance from him. Clearly, her instincts were entirely correct. He wasn't a good guy, had never been a good guy, and never would be a good guy.

"I ordered you the cheeseburger with ordinary fries. I hope that's okay." She handed him back his coffee.

"You don't have to be nervous."

"It's not exactly normal for a guy to be so interested in my bruise."

"Very true, but I'm not a normal guy. I never promised I was." He offered her a smile, hoping he looked harmless. Hard to do when he'd killed people without blinking.

"Right. Enjoy your coffee."

He watched her every move, and he admired her nice, round ass as she walked away. Ten minutes later she came back with his plate of food, and she left him to eat.

Maurice got back to him, along with a bill twice as much as he was expecting. Chains paid him by instant transfer, and opened up the file on his cell phone.

It always amazed him what Maurice could do with a name and a couple of clues. There wasn't anything anyone could hide from the hacker.

Lori Dean, twenty-five years old, came from a big family, and by big, he was talking one of ten siblings.

She was poor, dirt poor, and Maurice had also included a warning. The neighborhood where she lived had a known pimp who liked to beat the shit out of the women.

Just seeing that warning made Chains angry.

He knew how she'd gotten the bruise, and it had just sealed Lori's fate.

****

Lori stared at her reflection, and slowly ran her finger underneath her eye, wincing as she did. It hurt being hit, and, checking to make sure the door was locked, she slowly opened her very tight uniform. She'd asked several times for a larger size, but her boss wouldn't budge. He told her men liked to see tits on display.

If she could get a job elsewhere she'd have been gone already, but in this day and age, she couldn't be picky about where she worked. At least she didn't have to screw anyone.

Bruises covered her ribcage, and it hurt for her to take a deep breath. Her ribs weren't broken, but she was in so much pain.

This was what happened when you told Carlton Riggs "no". She wasn't an idiot. Carlton Riggs was a pimp, drug dealer, small arms dealer, asshole, bastard, and just everything that was bad in the world.

A couple of the girls she'd gone to school with had thought they'd been the ones to catch his eye, only to find themselves pregnant, and at his mercy. He didn't treat the mothers of his children any differently. To get any kind of money from him, they had to do it on their backs, serving anyone who'd have them, screwing travelers in the backs of cars, or serving men he wanted to entertain.

She'd seen the two girls she'd gone to school with the other day, and instead of looking like healthy twenty-five-year-olds, they looked twenty years older, and were miserable.

Carlton was also the reason for her bruised face and ribs.

Her parents loved fucking like rabbits, and because of that, they had a family of twelve. She had some older brothers, but none of them cared about feeding the younger kids that were still in school. She did. At the grocery store, she'd bumped into Carlton, where he'd promised her easy cash.

Once again, she'd turned him down. She didn't want to be a whore. Her body was her own, and it still filled her with pride that she was a virgin, even at twenty-five. Being around sex all of her life, she'd not been in any hurry to lose her V-card, and was happy with it.

She was going to hurt for another few days, so she buttoned up her uniform, tied back her brown hair, and left the bathroom.

Entering the kitchen, she saw George, the owner and cook, staring out at the seating area.

"That guy in the suit. Makes sure he gets everything he wants. Show him a smile, and he'll tip you good. Didn't he want the chicken?"

He didn't see her wince. George never cooked chicken for long enough, and whenever she could, she always advised their customers not to order it. She was surprised the health department hadn't closed them down.

She'd warned him about it, and he told her to shut her trap, that she didn't have the first clue what she was talking about.

Seeing as she needed the job, she did shut her mouth, and just kept on doing what she did best, serving customers, and faking a smile and happiness.

"He didn't want the chicken."

"Do you think he'll want the pie?" he asked.

"I don't know. He's still eating, so I'll wait to go and check."

She took the refilled pot of coffee, and as she went to pass George, he grabbed her arm, stalling her.

"I don't want to scare away the customers. Your face isn't going to bring trouble here, is it?"

"No. It won't."

"I mean it, Lori. I'm not interested in getting into

trouble."

"You won't. I promise." She stared at his hand on her, and he released her.

She didn't see Carlton coming here. If she did, she'd no longer work here anyway, as she wanted to be far away from where she grew up. Lori had only been in the old neighborhood grocery store to get food for her younger siblings. They were always on her mind, even though the youngest was now a teenager.

Carlton tended to stay around the streets that he controlled rather than venture out. She worried about her younger sisters, always warning them to steer clear of Carlton and his gang.

Leaving the kitchen, she made her way to one table where a little girl asked her for a chocolate milkshake. She put the coffee pot down, made the milkshake, and smiled at the young girl, remembering being that girl.

Whenever she was out with her brothers and sisters she'd always tried to get them treats if she could afford it. Most of her wages had gone to her parents back then, not that they seemed to remember her. She'd put the money in the pot in the kitchen, where they always stored their money. Half the time she was sure her parents forgot she even existed between all of their kids. It was lonely.

Lori continued her rounds. She held the coffee up. "Would you like some more coffee?"

"Yes." The man in the suit put his cup in front of him, and she poured him some coffee.

"Why is your cook constantly staring at me? Did he spit in my food?"

She smiled. "No. He didn't spit in your food. He wants to know if you'd like a piece of pie, and he wants me to smile a lot at you for an extra tip."

Even though he had a shaved head, she found him to be incredibly handsome. A cross between Dwayne Johnson and Vin Diesel, but his own unique look. The suit couldn't hide the muscles it covered. His arms were huge. She was sure they were as big as her thighs, and being the fat girl, she had large, chunky thighs.

"Is his pie worth it?"

"I'd go for his cherry pie. It's really nice with vanilla ice cream."

Her stomach chose that moment to growl, and heat filled her cheeks. She hadn't eaten that day, and she was now suffering for it.

"Take a fry," he said.

"No, that's your food."

"Lori, do me a favor and eat the fry. I'll have the pie with the ice cream, but I won't if you don't eat."

She rolled her eyes, and took a fry. Biting down, she appreciated the sweet gesture even though the fry was completely cold.

"And another one."

"Don't you want to eat?" she asked.

"I've been told I'm getting pie."

She chuckled, and took another fry. After standing with him for a few minutes, she held her hands up. "I've got to go and give coffee to others. I hope you enjoy your meal."

"I'm enjoying the company more."

Was he flirting with her?

She didn't know, as she was a plain girl and rarely did anyone flirt with her. She was the kind of woman that everyone overlooked, bland and not important.

"You can come and sit with me if there's a lull."

This new customer kept trying to tempt her to spend some time with him, and each time, she refused.

George would skin her alive if she sat down on the job.

She looked behind her as he watched her, and she liked his gaze on her body. In a weird kind of way, she felt him actually look at her, seeing her for who she was. The attention was nice for a change.

No one really took a good, long look or cared enough to see her.

Lori didn't know his name, and once he left, she knew she'd never see him again.

Serving the rest of the customers, she actually felt like smiling even with her bruised eye.

She couldn't recall the last time she'd been happy.

It wouldn't last, but for now, she'd keep those depressing thoughts aside.

George already had the pie and ice cream ready, and she served the man. She didn't know the man's name, but being near him made her feel happy, safe, and at times a little scared. There was something about the way he looked at her. The intense look that made her think of a wolf with a sheep in his sights.

Those nerves kept her at a distance.

Of course, he didn't stay forever, and she found herself glancing toward where he'd been sitting, wondering who he was, his name, everything. The empty booth brought out one of those fleeting moments of regret that she squashed just as quickly as it came.

The rest of her shift went by without any hiccups. No one else flirted with her or wanted to know her better. She went through the motions until it was time to clock off.

She grabbed her bags, and was about to leave the diner, not paying attention to anything, until George called her back.

"I don't suppose you'd throw this outside in the

dumpster?" He held up a large black garbage bag.

George would never be a gentleman, but not wanting to piss off her boss, she took the bag and lugged it into the darkened alley.

She hated the back alley, especially at night. It reminded her of every horror movie she'd ever watched. As she threw the bag in to the trash, she gasped as someone wrapped an arm around her waist, pressing a cloth against her nose.

Panic washed over her, and she fought, screaming. With every passing second, her body grew lax, and then little by little, her eyes closed as sleep claimed her.

## Chapter Two

She was still out cold.

Chains sat in the folding chair, watching the gentle rise and fall of her chest. A sleeping angel. He'd been sitting next to her, lost in thought, for over an hour. He didn't regret his choice to bring her here. It was for her own damn good. The world out there would eat her alive, and this was the only place he could keep her safe.

He'd never had much growing up. In the hierarchy of the orphanage and later the local Russian mafia, he only got the scraps. That was a long time ago. A lifetime he'd gladly forget. Now Chains had choices, made his own rules. And this little lamb was his prize. Only his, and nobody could ever take her from him.

In all his years since moving over from his motherland, he'd never taken an interest in a woman. They were good for one thing. Otherwise, they were in his way. He wasn't sure what it was about this one—*Lori Dean*. Maybe it was the vulnerability in her eyes, the bruise, or something triggered from his past. All he knew for certain was he couldn't walk away. Something deep inside him, in the dark recesses of his soul, demanded he protect her from herself, to keep her as his treasure.

Before he even left the diner, his plan was already in action. The voice in his head told him to take her, and he was in complete agreement. He knew Boss would never condone him kidnapping a young woman and chaining her in his basement, but nobody would know except him. Lori would be his dirty little secret.

Chains rolled out his shoulders. He still had time before she woke up, so he decided to get some of the wheels of his plan in motion. When his little houseguest woke up, she wouldn't be happy, so he wanted to have something to offer her. A peace offering. Since he already wanted to gut the asshole who dared to put his hands on her, it was going to be a good move regardless.

He had enough intel from Maurice's initial report on Lori to track down the local bad boy. He was twenty-nine, skinny, covered in ink. Apparently, he ruled the neighborhood with an iron fist, the cause of undue fear and suffering in the small community. It was all going to end very soon. Little shits like Carlton Riggs were small potatoes to anyone working for Killer of Kings, but Chains was going to enjoy this kill personally.

Chains stood up and stared down at Lori one more time. He'd taken the elastic from her hair and removed that polyester uniform top she'd been wearing. That's when he noticed the extent of her bruising. It wasn't just her eye, but most of her chest. What kind of lowlife prick picked on a woman? Just looking at her injuries made his muscles tense, violent thoughts clamoring in his head. He wanted answers. Why had Carlton put his hands on Lori in the first place?

He made his way upstairs, securing the basement door after him. His eyes adjusted to the brighter lighting as he slipped on one of his custom gun holsters. Boss ensured he always had the latest toys and gadgets for killing and recon. The past few years he'd been doing more driving and intel for the owner of Killer of Kings. Boss trusted him, and that said a lot. When heavy shit went down, Chains was one of the first men he called.

After strapping himself with heat, he pulled on a jacket. Unlike most of the crew he worked with, Chains wasn't covered in ink, so he had the ability to slip in and out of a crowd without attracting too much attention. In fact, his skin was unmarred by a single tattoo. When he'd been recruited into his first low-ranking mafia after aging out of his orphanage, they'd branded him like a fucking dog with their insignia. He'd worked as a *krysha*, doing shakedowns and cheap hits in exchange for nothing more than meals. Being on the bottom of the food chain in a basement Russian mafia was a special kind of hell. It took a few years, but Chains ended up with more skills and balls than their leader and took out all the top players single-handedly before moving onto bigger leagues.

He'd cut that brand off with a pocket knife, and still had the gnarly scar on his shoulder to prove it. Until this day, he'd never allowed any ink on his body. His body was his own.

Chains drove out to Lori's old stomping grounds. The neighborhood looked like shit, and "ghetto" would have been a compliment. Since joining Killer of Kings, Chains had learned to enjoy the finer things in life. Money, status, and firearms meant he had choices. He valued his freedom, his independence, and the fact he'd never be on the bottom again.

He pulled his car around to the rear of a community center. It was after hours, so he expected the unsavory crowd out back. Dark shadows lingered around the figures, only one lone light by the back door and a distant street light providing illumination. He rolled down his window, the slow crunch of gravel beneath his tires mingling with laughter and cursing.

A man in a hood approached the driver's side.

"I'm looking for Carlton," said Chains

"You buying?"

"Sure."

"What do you need?"

Chains took a cleansing breath, his patience already wearing thin. "I said I wanted to deal with Carlton, not you."

The man straightened up, then whistled towards one of the larger crowds. Weed was pungent in the air, the deep bass from a distant car another distraction to his benefit. When three men approached, he couldn't make them out, just their silhouettes. He knew the one in the middle was Carlton, just from his arrogant stride.

"What is it?" asked Carlton.

"This guy's looking to buy. He'll only talk to you."

Carlton rested his forearm on the hood on Chains's car and leaned in close. He reeked of alcohol and cigarettes. "Who the fuck are you?"

"Get in. We have business we need to discuss," said Chains, still looking straight out the windshield.

"I don't know you."

"Well, I hear you're the one who calls the shots around here, so you're the only man who matters." Chains knew the big-headed prick would thrive off praise, and he was right.

"Jimmy, come with me."

Carlton got in the passenger seat, and Jimmy sat in the backseat, both doors slamming shut simultaneously. Chains rolled up his window, pleased he had his prey securely in his web. Tonight would be a good night.

"Okay, what the fuck is all this about?" asked Carlton. "I don't have all night."

Chains was finished with his charade. He clicked the door lock button, ensuring no one left his car until he said so.

"Do you remember Lori Dean?"

"What? Who? What the fuck is this?"

"Lori Dean, twenty-five-year-old waitress. You beat the shit out of her this week. Still haven't jogged your memory?"

Carlton tried the door handle, panicking when he couldn't open it. "Open the fucking door? Who the hell are you?"

"I'm not opening the door until you tell me why you hit her."

"Fuck you." Carlton nodded to the big guy in the backseat, and a handgun cocked near Chains's temple. The sound made his dick hard. These fuckers had no idea of the world of hurt coming their way. "Now. Open the damn door."

Chains twisted in his seat, grabbing Jimmy's wrist with one hand and dropping the other elbow down hard into the man's forearm. His moves were so fast, within two seconds the man's own gun was pointing in his face. Chains pulled the trigger.

He dropped back down in his seat, shifted into reverse and then slammed on the gas. The car whirled and skidded around in the lot before he was back on the main road. Carlton was in shock, his hands in a death grip with the dashboard and door handle. Chains headed to the edge of town where it was heavily wooded and then stopped the car in a dark grove.

"Who are you?"

"You don't get to ask questions, Carlton Riggs. You only answer mine. Do you understand?"

"Okay. Sure. Whatever."

"Why did you put your hands on Lori Dean?"

He chuckled nervously, tweaking in his seat. "I barely even remember that chick. She was getting groceries for her sisters and brothers. I only offered her money."

"In return for what?"

"Look, I run a business here. Some guys are into fat chicks. She could make me some money and help her family. Win-win."

"But she refused you, didn't she?"

"Yeah, the stupid bitch."

Chains punched him in the mouth, his body

slamming back against the passenger door from the impact. Carlton touched the blood on his lip.

"Why'd you hit her?"

He was breathing heavily now, probably realizing the shit situation he was in. "To teach her a lesson."

"It's your word or the highway, right?"

"I own this town. If she didn't like it, she shouldn't have come back. She hire you or something?"

Chains shook his head. "She doesn't know I'm here." He wondered what trophy he could bring for her. Something to prove the bastard who'd hurt her was dead. Maybe a finger? A pic on his cellphone?

"I don't understand."

He shifted in his seat, facing Carlton. "There are some men out there that don't believe you should hit an innocent woman. Ever. You're obviously not one of them."

"I have no beef with you. What do you want? Money? Drugs?"

He scoffed. "Revenge."

Carlton tried to forcibly open the door, finally reaching into his boot for a blade, holding it up in front of him. "Open the door and let me out."

"Sure, I can do that."

Chains released the locks, then got out of the car. Carlton ran ahead, his lanky body highlighted by the headlamps. He fell down once in his panic to get away. Chains pushed his lapels open and pulled out one of his Glocks, taking his time to screw on a silencer. He shot Carlton in the calf, watching him drop to the dust at the side of the road.

"Get your ass back here or the next one's a head shot." Chains sat on the hood, waiting for him to hobble over with only one good leg. When he was close enough, he added, "Get your friend out of my backseat."

Once the dead body was dumped at the edge of the forest, Chains instructed Carlton to drag it deeper into the woods. He checked his watch, and knew he had to get back to his house soon. Lori would be waking from the drugs soon, and he didn't want her to panic.

This was all for her.

"Okay, done. Now, please, let me go," Carlton said.

Chains approached him, punching him in the eye, knocking him to the ground. In his orphanage, he'd been the runt when he was a kid, but he'd always been a fighter. Now he had the bulk and muscle to back himself up. Sometimes it felt good to use his fists instead of a blade or gun, like now, as he gave this punk a taste of his own medicine.

"How did that feel?"

"Stay away from me."

"I'm not done with you. Lori had bruises on her chest, and I'm a firm believer of an eye for an eye," said Chains.

He straddled Carlton's prone body, crouched low, and gave him the same treatment he'd given Lori. When he finally stood back up, the pimp was sputtering blood.

"No more..."

Chains squatted near Carlton's head. "I should apologize. I may have led you to believe I was some kind of outstanding citizen, you know, watching out for women abused by piece of shit drug dealers. But that's about as far as my civilities extend. Unfortunately for you, I've never been too good with compassion for my enemies. And when you put your hands on Lori, you became my enemy."

"What are you going to do?"

"You're not listening." Chains twisted the man's ear until he cried out. "Nobody touches my woman and lives."

**** 

Lori coughed, the musty scent irritating her throat, and remembered how much her chest still hurt. She opened her eyes and a wave of dizziness took her by surprise, so she closed them again.

*Where am I?*

She tried to focus her thoughts, to remember the last sequence of events, but came up short. Then she remembered George nagging her about the garbage. That was the last thing she remembered. No, there was more. She remembered struggling in arms stronger than steel.

Lori bolted up into a sitting position, her adrenaline high rushing through her veins. It was too dark to see clearly, only a small nightlight giving the faintest glow. When she moved her arms, the clang of chains startled her. Both her wrists had wide cuffs with chains dangling from them.

It was too quiet. All she could hear was her breathing. Could there be another person in the room? Lori was too afraid to even whisper.

She stood up and pulled the lengths of chain taut, discovering she was attached to a wall. Her heart hammered in her chest. She stepped up on the padded bench she'd been asleep on, trying to pry the metal loops from the concrete block wall. She kept digging and picking at the fastening and links in the chain until her nails chipped away.

*This can't be happening to me.*

She dropped back down, too scared and confused to cry. That's when she noticed she was wearing her sports bra and had no clue where her uniform was. Lori began to pat herself down, relieved that her skirt was still on and nothing felt out of sorts between her legs. Still, whatever was happening was not looking in her favor.

She'd been kidnapped.

Was it Carlton Riggs? Had he found her at the diner? Was he going to rape and kill her, beat her until she agreed to sell her body? Maybe it was a serial killer, and he planned to torture her until her final breath. Now she began to cry. No scenario ended well for her.

Her fears and desperation had reached the boiling point. She couldn't believe her bad luck. All her life had been a struggle—for food, love, security, money. Nothing came easy, and this was how it would all end?

She stood and yanked at the chains, leaning all her weight back, pulling until her wrists were raw. What did she have to lose? She had to escape before her captor returned. When the chains wouldn't give, her panic level increased. She dropped down to her knees, crawling in the dark as she attempted to find anything to use as a weapon or escape tool. Lori patted the cold concrete floor to the full extent her chains would allow, coming up empty.

She struggled with her bonds, yelling and crying until everything was gone.

No more tears.

No more anger.

No more hope.

A door whined open, the flood of light from the top of a long staircase momentarily blinding her. She sat up, then crouched low at the end of the bench, trying to remain hidden, even though it wouldn't do her any good. Lori's brain was on overdrive. She wondered what she could bargain with, but she had no money, nothing of value, and nobody would notice she was gone. George would notice at opening shift tomorrow, but he'd write her off and have a "now hiring" sign up within the hour.

She peeked over the top of the bench and watched the black booted feet slowly descend, each step punctuated with a creak in the wooden stairs. Her mouth was dry, her hands trembling. Just before the man's face appeared, she ducked back down, praying to stay invisible.

"What the fuck?"

A lamp flicked on, a soft glow lighting the basement. Lori let out a little gasp. Her instinct was to slap her hand over her mouth, but she dared not move and rattle her chains. She kept her focus on the cracks in the grey concrete, and watched a potato bug try to bury itself under the leg of the bench. She wished she could disappear so easily.

Heavy footsteps came closer. She counted the steps, wondering if it was possible to die from fear itself.

"What have you done to yourself?" The deep voice was vaguely familiar, but she was too messed up to make sense of anything right now. "Lori?"

Her name registered, and that's when she knew her kidnapper knew her, planned this for whatever twisted reason. It had to be Carlton. She wasn't on anyone else's radar.

When his hands wrapped around her upper arms, she screamed and struggled, kicking out her legs until they hit the wall. The chains rattled violently. Her eyes were tightly closed, as if not witnessing any more would somehow make things better.

"Help me!" she yelled. Maybe someone upstairs would have pity on her. Maybe a passerby would hear her screams.

"Damn it, Lori. Stop it! You're only hurting yourself."

"Help!"

The beast of a man holding her had had enough. He sat down on the bench with her on his lap, her arms immobilized at her sides. There was no use struggling, and eventually she lost all her steam.

"Look at your wrists, for God's sake." He ran the pad of his thumb along the raw areas, and she flinched on contact. "I'm not going to hurt you."

She wanted to ask questions, but didn't dare open her mouth. Lori was certain she wouldn't like the answers.

"Are you hungry?"

The last thing she cared about right now was food.

"Okay, first things first. I need to get these cuffs off and bandage up your wrists. I don't know what the fuck I was thinking using chains on you." He stood up and positioned her on the bench. Her captor bent down on one knee in front of her. "Lori, look at me."

She didn't want to look at him. Witnessing the enemy was a surefire way to seal her fate. But disobeying could be worse in her predicament. Lori took a little breath and looked at the man in front of her. Her jaw dropped.

It was him.

Cherry pie man.

She'd been fantasizing about him all night before her shift ended. He'd been the first man to give her attention, and there'd been something dark and appealing about him. Oh, how she'd pegged him wrong. She tried to remember everything he'd said, she'd said, and how on earth she could talk herself out of this nightmare.

He touched her eye, a feather-light caress. "No man will ever hurt you again."

She wasn't sure what it was—the sound of his voice or the way he said the words—but she believed him.

## Chapter Three

Okay, so maybe he should have anticipated her freaking out, but still, Chains wasn't going to hurt her. She was precious to him, and he had no intention of her ever suffering again. Not at his hands or anyone else's. She belonged to him now.

Her gaze roamed up the length of his body, and he saw the tears in her eyes, the confusion.

"You're from the diner," she said. Her voice sounded hoarse.

"You shouldn't scream. There's no one around for miles, and no one to hear you. It's kind of pointless."

He saw her lip wobble, and he cursed. That one word made her flinch, and he gritted his teeth. Damn it. He wasn't good at this kind of stuff. Years of being treated like shit, and here he was, stealing a girl that deep down, he knew he shouldn't have—yet couldn't seem to deny himself.

For too long he'd always been told what to do, and the moment he saw Lori, and saw the pain she carried, he had to take her away from all that shit, and help her. No one had been there to help him.

He tucked some stray hairs behind her ear. She leaned away from his touch, and he frowned. Chains expected this to go much smoother.

"I don't understand what's going on."

"The man who hurt you." She flinched, and he wished that he could go back and kill the bastard all over the again. Considering Carlton had been the king of his little street, he'd screamed like a fucking bitch while he'd tortured him. The sounds he made hadn't been pretty. "He's not going to hurt you anymore."

She frowned. "You mean Carlton?"

"Yes."

"Wait, how did you know about that?"

"I have means of finding out anything that I need." He wanted to reach out and touch her skin, but held back.

*You've kidnapped her.*

*Don't freak her out with more.*

She looked away, and the crease on her forehead got deeper. Her mind was probably on overdrive, plotting how to get away from her kidnapper.

He was supposed to be the fucking hero.

Chains massaged her wrists, hating the red sores that were already forming. She'd been pulling on the chains, and he didn't think to cushion them. Never expected any of this.

"I'll be back." Leaving his spot, he made his way back up into his kitchen, and found the first aid kit. He went to the sitting room, opened a drawer, and pulled out some foam as a precaution.

At the first opportunity Lori was going to run. He knew that, but he wasn't going to let her.

When he entered the basement this time, he locked the door, and pocketed the key before making his way back down. She still sat in the same position he'd left her in, frozen in place. Her arms rested on her knees, wrists exposed, and he hated seeing the chain marks marring her pale skin. She was a beautiful woman, and didn't deserve this kind of treatment.

"Are you going to kill me?" she whispered. Tears fell down her cheeks when she looked up at him. Such innocence. All his.

"No, I'm not going to kill you." He took a seat, and pulled out the key to her cuff. When he released one of the bands, she quickly held her wrist to her chest. She winced as she rubbed the mark. "You're going to hurt yourself. Let me take care of you. While I do this, you can ask as many questions as you like."

He saw the temptation in her eyes. She wanted to know more. She needed to understand what was going on, and as each second passed, not knowing drove her crazy. He knew what she felt more than she could ever know. Just hearing the clang of the chains brought back memories from his past. It was how he'd gotten his name. The other hitmen at Killer of Kings thought it was just a nickname, but it was steeped in a dark reality that he tried to forget.

"If you're not going to kill me, why am I here?"

"You're my reward."

"For what?"

"For a really fucked up life."

"You're going to rape me?" She pulled her hand away before he could even get a good look at it.

He stared at her. "No, I'm not going to rape you. I don't believe in hurting innocent women." She wouldn't give him her hand, and now he saw she was shaking. "Talk to me."

"I don't know what to say."

"You've got questions, ask them. Pretend we're at the diner."

"Easier said than done. It's kind of hard to think of all the right questions because I'm a lot freaked out right now."

"I'll do my best to answer anything you want."

He still held his hand out, the ointment on his other fingers. When he was on a job, his patience would often be tested, but right now, he felt an overwhelming sense of calm and patience just by being in her presence.

"Let me have your wrist so I can protect it."

Slowly, she lowered her wrist, and he held her arm. He began to treat the wound, careful as he rubbed the cream into her wrist. At his first touch, she flinched, and he didn't mind. Everyone who didn't know they were safe, always flinched. She was just being human. Chains, on the other hand, had lost his humanity in the slums of Kapotnya. He didn't flinch anymore.

"This doesn't make any sense at all."

"In what way?" he asked.

"You've kidnapped me. Now you're treating my wounds. I don't get it. It doesn't make sense," she said.

He smiled. "You've said that twice now."

"I don't know what to think. All my life, when I've read and heard stories of women being kidnapped, they're usually found days, weeks, or months later. They're raped, tortured, or brutally murdered. I don't want to die. I have a really shitty life. Probably one that makes people think I don't want to live, but I do. I have so many plans."

"What kind of plans?" he asked. Chains never cared about the women he fucked. He wanted to know everything about Lori Dean.

He finished with one cuff, and moved onto the next, treating her wrist. The tension in her body had eased slightly, so that was a good sign.

"I don't know. I hoped to one day go to college, but because I was too busy looking after my brothers and sisters, I didn't graduate high school. I was going to take night classes, but my parents needed all the money they could get their hands on."

He was aware of her financial situation, and the fact she dropped out of high school. "You need to stop worrying about your parents and their kids. They're not your responsibility."

"But if I don't care about them, who will?" she asked. "I don't want them to have the same experiences as me."

"I know they're your brothers and sisters, but you

didn't give birth to them. Your parents did, and they should be the ones to care. If they don't, they've got ways and means of dealing with all of them."

Her eyes glistened with fresh tears. "You mean go into care, right? The foster system where everyone gets forgotten. And probably much worse."

Chains saw her pain, and it cut him deep to know she cared so much for her siblings. He'd never cared about anyone, because nobody ever cared about him. She was right though. Foster care was bullshit.

"I can't let that happen. They don't deserve it," she said.

"And you deserve to lose your life because your parents couldn't use protection? Think about it, Lori, all you're doing is taking care of kids that aren't yours. You're enabling them to have more because they know they're going to get taken care of. When was the last time someone ran you a bubble bath, or took care of you when you felt sick?

Those tears came full force now, and she released a sob.

"You may think you're not worth all that much, but you know what? I think you are, and you deserve a lot fucking better than what they've been giving you." He reached up and tucked some hair behind her ear. "Now, you could try and see this as a vacation."

"A vacation?"

"I'm going to take care of you, Lori. No one's been taking care of you. Even that fucking manager of yours needs to be taught a lesson, making you take the trash down a darkened alley like that. If it hadn't been me, it would have been someone, and then what would you have done?" he asked.

She frowned. "You shouldn't have taken me in the first place."

"How about you give it a week?" he asked, more than willing to compromise to earn her trust.

"A week?"

"Yes. Allow me to show you what it would be like to be taken care of, and in the meantime, you don't try to run, or to escape. We'll see what happens."

"You know this is completely crazy, right? This isn't what kidnappers do."

"The way you keep talking about real kidnappers, it's as if you want me to actually hurt you." She'd watched too many horror flicks. Then again, some of the scenes left behind by Killer of Kings would give her real nightmares.

"No, I don't want to be hurt."

He smiled. He wouldn't have hurt her even if she begged. "What do you think?" he asked.

She glanced around the basement, and then looked down at herself. "Do I at least get to shower during this week?"

"Yes, you've got to promise that you won't try to run though. My house is built like Fort fucking Knox. You're not getting out, and if you try, I'll chain you back down here so you don't hurt yourself." He'd left her uncuffed and waited. "One week where all of your needs are met. I'll even cook for you. I'm pretty good at that. I've got movies and books. A week to worry about you, no responsibilities."

She nibbled her lip, and he saw her waver.

"I won't touch you, so don't worry about that. There's no one else in the house, either. What do you say?"

\*\*\*\*

He was the worst kidnapper in the world.

Lori nodded her head. One week of not having to worry about going to work, getting home, buying groceries to feed her siblings, and dealing with whatever chaos her parents had found themselves in was just too much temptation.

She'd probably have to worry about a new job now and how she'd make up a week's worth of expenses, but she wasn't really in a position to change her situation. Chains waited as she climbed off the bench, and padded across the cold floor toward the stairs. He opened the door, and she followed him out into a huge luxury kitchen with natural wood cabinetry. The room had to be bigger than her entire one-room apartment.

She glanced at the door, and the craziest thing of all, she wasn't even tempted to run. From eight years old, she'd been taking care of her brothers and sisters. Getting them ready for school and always being the constant in their lives. She'd learned how to read fast so that she could tell them a bedtime story, and would use library books as her parents didn't exactly care for reading material in the house.

There hadn't been any free time to play. All she'd ever known was children and work. The stress, the demands, the responsibilities were all too much, and even before cherry pie man showed up, she'd been at the breaking point.

"What's your name?" she asked.

Had he told her it? She didn't know. Her head was a mess.

Between being kidnapped, the confusion, and now the temptation of a relaxing week, she must have forgotten it.

"It's Chains."

She rubbed at her wrists, thinking about the chains she'd just come out of.

"Follow me."

They left the kitchen, and it opened up into a

large hallway. The furniture was elegant, and everything professionally decorated, unlike her parents' place. Her childhood home was complete with peeling wallpaper, threadbare furniture, and they didn't even have a whole carpet. Floorboards peeked through, and she was sure there was a resident rat, but she could never find it. Half the time they couldn't even afford to keep the heat on.

"You have a nice home," she said. "Kidnapping must be very lucrative. Unfortunately, you picked one of the poorest women you could find this time."

"You're my first victim." He smiled. "Trust me, I never expected to live like this."

She wanted to know more. "Why?"

"When you come from nothing, it's hard to imagine having anything in life. No one ever really wants to help you out, do they? Everyone's in it for themselves. You should know," he said.

She did. No one had cared about what she was going through. They'd all just wanted her to deal with it, and move on.

Chains didn't linger long on the main floor. They headed up a very sturdy wooden staircase with decorative carvings, and she held onto the banister, wondering what he did for a living. There was a lot more to him than just sitting in a diner and eating cherry pie. This kind of luxury, he should have been at one of those fancy restaurants, the kind with caviar and truffles, not a greasy spoon.

They came to the far hallway, and his hand was on the door. "This is going to be your room for the next week."

He opened the door, and she didn't know what she expected, but it was like out of a fairy tale. A large four-poster bed, a dressing table, so much space, and the air smelled fresh. Not of damp, decay, and piss. She spun around, and she couldn't keep the smile off her face. Was this a joke?

"This here is your wardrobe, and I'll deal with getting you some clothes that you like. En-suite bathroom. There's a robe and towels in there." He moved to take a seat on the edge of the bed. "Go ahead. Check it out."

"I can shower in there?"

"You can even have a bath if you'd like."

She nodded, and went inside. Everything took her breath away, it was so beautiful. The mix of modern and old-world design was breathtaking, like something out of a home and garden magazine.

Running a bath, she found lavender-scented bath salts, and sprinkled some in the bath, along with bubbles.

She didn't feel comfortable removing her clothes. No matter how many promises Chains made, he'd still kidnapped her. She couldn't put her guards down. At least he hadn't beaten her. All he'd done was knock her out with some chloroform, which sounded bad, but it wasn't anything compared to what Carlton had done to her.

"What kind of food do you like?" He leaned against the doorframe, and this time she really paid attention. When he'd been in the diner, he'd worn a full suit. Now he only had a navy t-shirt and black jeans. His shoulders were huge, and the muscles in his arms flexed when he crossed them.

"What do you mean?"

"I'm going to order us some takeout. Chinese, Mexican, Italian? What do you love?"

"I'd love to try some Chinese food," she said.

"You've never tried it before?"

"No." She'd always wanted to, but her parents hated it, and said not to waste money on something they wouldn't eat.

"I'll order the menu."

She was sure she heard him wrong. For a second, she thought about her responsibilities. The guilt began to gnaw at her, and she was tempted to make a run for it.

*One week.*

She didn't know what would happen after that week, but she couldn't help but think and feel that Chains was right. Her brothers and sisters were not her responsibility. For too long, and too often, it had just been assumed that she would deal with them.

*"Lori, go get cough medicine."*

*"Lori, wake up, and feed your brother. We're tired."*

*"Lori, you can't go to school today."*

*"Lori, don't be so selfish, and take care of your sister."*

Sitting on the edge of the bathtub, she couldn't think of a single reason why she should go back home. To her apartment. To her old life. Everyone used her. Did they even for a second worry where she might be? Or were they just pissed off that Lori wasn't there to deal with their kids?

Tears filled her eyes once again, not from fear, but a deep-seated sadness.

"You're crying," Chains said. "Why are you crying? Are you hurt?"

It was all just too much. A complete stranger had cared more for her in the past few minutes than her own parents had. And her own fate wasn't even certain.

"I'm fine."

"That doesn't sound fine. Please, Lori, let me help you."

He hadn't even entered the room.

He was giving her space, taking care of her, and

loving her in a way that her own parents had failed to do.

This was probably going against every single warning or alarm bell going off inside her head, but she asked for him to enter.

He stepped into the room, and he didn't leer at her. The concern etched on his face touched her heart.

"What's the matter?" he asked, moving a little closer.

"You care," she said.

Her words seemed to stop him in his tracks. "I'm confused."

"Do you know how long I've wanted something like this? To have someone see me, and to care? It's something from romance novels, not reality." She didn't even mind when he took a seat on the edge of the bathtub near her. He'd promised he wouldn't hurt her, and in some crazy way, she believed him. He'd not hurt her once. "I've done everything all my life, and I'm tired. I'm always so tired, and it's hard that a complete stranger would care enough to help me." She touched her face, and winced.

"Your parents didn't do that," he said.

"They didn't, but if the guy who did had come to our place, it makes me wonder what they'd have made me do to keep him out." She sniffled.

"I don't like to see you cry."

"I'm having a wakeup call right now."

"How do you mean?" he asked.

"I always thought in some weird kind of way that my parents loved me. That they cared, and now I see I was just the help to them. I was a kid that looked after their other kids, and now, they're probably annoyed that I didn't bring them my tips. They don't care at all."

"I care," he said. "I care about what happens to you, and no one is ever going to harm you. Don't even worry about the guy that did that to your face. I took care of him."

She didn't know what that meant. Had he called the cops? Carlton was dangerous, even for a man like Chains. She didn't want to push her luck by delving deeper, so she just nodded.

"Thank you."

"I'm not very good at feelings, but with you, I'll try." Chains stared at her. "The world is an ugly place, and I found a beautiful start to stare at."

Heat filled her cheeks. It was so sweet of him to say so.

"I'm not beautiful."

"You are to me. When I was a kid I'd often wish on the stars, hoping to have a better life. Praying for something more. When nothing changed, I'd pray for something else. Seemed like an endless cycle, like God had forgotten me."

"What did you pray for?" she asked, curious. Other women would be trying to find a way out of this mess. She found herself drawn to this man, and it wasn't because he'd taken her. He was … attentive.

"I prayed for something to call my own." The sound of the doorbell ringing interrupted their conversation. "Food's here."

He got up and left.

He never touched her. She'd talked, and he'd listened.

Wiping the tears from her face, she closed the bathroom door and slipped into the waiting bath. She washed her body and hair quickly and then stood up, reaching for the robe. She tied her hair up in a towel and stared at herself in the mirror. She was twenty-five and felt much older. Her life was slipping away as she lived for everyone but herself. Her eye was still a deep purple hue, and it was a constant reminder of the life she wanted no part of.

When she entered the bedroom, Chains was already there. "Food's in the dining room."

Her stomach chose that moment to growl, and he chuckled.

"I've been neglecting my duties." He held his hand out.

Any sane woman would ignore the hand. She took it, and felt completely safe as he led her down to dinner.

## Chapter Four

*One week later*

Chains studied his reflection as he scraped the blade along his jawline. He'd always shaved with a straight razor rather than the new disposable ones. Some things shouldn't be messed with.

He rinsed his razor off and set it aside before splashing water on his face. When he looked back up at himself, he wasn't sure what the fuck he saw.

*What have you done?*

Everything had been going so well, too well, with Lori. After the third day, she started to get squirrely, questioning her confinement, and worrying about bills and her siblings. That's when he had to return her to his basement.

Chains wasn't sure what he expected. It's not like he planned on kidnapping her. It all happened so fast, his decision made on instinct. One he still didn't regret, even though he knew he should.

His chloroform was for marks with contracts on their heads. He was mixing business and pleasure, and Boss would have his head if he found out.

Nobody knew the real Chains, and maybe he didn't even know himself. His entire social life was an act. He was never on anyone's radar, not even Boss's. When he was on assignment, the other men at Killer of Kings assumed he was just one of the guys, carefree, competent at his job.

Yes, he did his job well. Killing was in his blood. But that's where their assumptions failed. The mask Chains wore for the world was a veneer to hide the darkness within. Recon and fulfilling contracts kept his mind busy, kept the demons at bay. Since before he could remember, his life had been a game of survival, selling his soul just to stay alive. Many of the experiences he'd lived through were mercifully blocked out of his mind, but they still shaped him into the monster he was today.

But since being hired on at Killer of Kings, he wanted more, wanted all he'd been denied. He overindulged in everything from women to cars. Chains demanded the best, like somehow the material possessions would make up for a bullshit life. It was all smoke and mirrors … until he saw Lori.

When he saw her, his needs became real. He deserved her, wanted her, and he wouldn't be denied. There was a piece of his past swirling in her eyes. He could see right through her exterior down to the pain, the burden, the desperation. She needed saving, and he wanted to be her hero. She'd been the one thing he'd prayed for most of his life. His own shining star.

His cellphone rang, so he grabbed a towel and dried his face as he returned to his bedroom. The cell was lying on the bed.

"Yeah."

"Vacation's over," said Boss. "I need you to handle the El Diablo situation."

He exhaled his irritation before speaking. "You too? The guy's name is Xavier. I'm not calling him El Diablo."

"Whatever. Just keep tabs on his movements. I want that fucker working for me."

Boss had a hard-on to hire Xavier ever since he knew about his past. The man was a killing machine, and good at it. If he wasn't so unstable, he could be the perfect fit, but then again, all the men at Killer of King were fucked up. Chains included.

Xavier had refused Boss's offer to join the organization during the showdown with Shadow and the mafia hit, but Boss wasn't ready to call it quits. He always got what he wanted. Chains already figured Boss was onto something that would bring Xavier to their side. Boss always told him that everyone had a weakness. All he needed was time to find Xavier's, if he didn't have it already.

"He's not new to this. He'll know I'm on to him."

"That's what I'm hoping. The information I have will make it too good for him to pass up," said Boss.

"Is that it?" He should have known Boss would already have something Xavier would want or need.

"Afraid not. I've emailed you the details on a new contract. Last minute situation. I need it done tonight."

He didn't like the idea of leaving Lori alone in the house for too long. Even though she was chained in his basement, he was trying his best to keep her comfortable. She was his secret toy, and he didn't want to share her with the world.

"I'll handle it," he said, not wanting to raise suspicions. Chains rarely refused Boss. The old bastard had given him a new lease on life. Boss had seen his potential when he'd been on a contract in Russia over a decade ago, and the rest was history.

A minute of silence followed. It felt like Boss could read his mind through the phone line. Chains ran a hand over his head as he waited.

"Everything okay?" asked Boss. Had Chains used a different tone? He'd tried hard not to give away anything, but Boss was ridiculously intuitive.

"Just feeling overwhelmed lately. Nothing I can't handle, though."

More silence. "I know where you came from. I'm the one to bring you here, remember that?"

"I remember."

"Well, you don't have to explain yourself to me.

The things you've been through are bound to haunt you," said Boss. "You've just got to bury that shit and not let it control you. Once you give it power, you're really fucked."

"I'm good."

"Check your email." Then Boss hung up.

Chains hadn't been bullshitting. Before he'd found Lori, he'd been at an all-time low. His killing desire had taken over. She'd saved him as much as he'd saved her.

A few days ago, he'd contemplating taking Lori's life. To make the problem he created go away. It's what he usually did. The internal battle had left a nice hole in his drywall. He couldn't hurt her. She was a victim, innocence personified, and it filled him with satisfaction to know she was safely under his roof. He just needed to keep control of himself, to not let his past define him, although it was easier said than done.

He finished dressing, black jeans and hoodie, then stopped by his weapons room. He pulled back the protective sheet on the center table and admired his collection. The email told him everything he needed to know. This was a quick find and eliminate, and within ten minutes, Maurice had the location. Now it was Chains's turn to kill. Just thinking about it filled him with a rush.

Chains had brought Lori her dinner an hour ago. He'd get her dishes and leave her some snacks.

He unlocked the basement door and took the stairs one by one. Lori was sitting on the bench reading one of the books he'd left for her. When she looked up at him, all his venom slipped away. "You all done with dinner?"

"I'm done," she said.

He squatted near her. "What are you reading

there?"

She rolled her eyes and set the book aside. "I don't need the books."

"It was just a question."

"What's going to happen to me, Chains?" Hearing her say his name was music to his ears. He wanted to hear her say it over and over again.

"I've already told you, I'll take care of you. If you hadn't been so difficult last week, you'd still have the run of the house."

She frowned, waving an arm in the air. "I know, why don't you put up some bars, and I'll be like a monkey in a cage. You can feed me bananas through the cracks."

Lori had been getting bolder each day. At least she had some fire. When he'd first taken her, she'd been broken and vulnerable. Her face was healing up nicely, only a light highlight under her eye where the worst of the punch had been.

"One day you'll appreciate what I'm doing for you. Maybe you'll thank me."

"Thank you for kidnapping me?"

"For saving you," he corrected. "You don't have to worry about Carlton since I killed him, do you?"

Her mouth fell agape. "W-what do you mean?"

"I'm not following."

"You said you *took care* of Carlton. Now you're saying you murdered him? Are you joking?"

Chains was confused. She sounded upset. How could she have an emotional response for a man who'd beaten her and made her life miserable?

"I don't understand why you're upset. Or shocked." He stood up and wandered around the basement. It had changed a lot since Lori arrived. He'd added more lighting, set up a twin bed, bookshelf, even a fake plant. Women liked that kind of shit. The bathroom only had a toilet and sink, so he'd let her upstairs later to shower or bathe.

"Murder? That's not normal." Then she got quiet, fiddling with her fingers.

*Fuck!* His intention wasn't to scare her. He wanted her to trust him.

He sat beside her, and she shifted away. Chains grabbed her arm and held her steady. "Listen, little lady, I killed that asshole because he put his hands on you. I'd do it again if I had to. Nobody touches what's mine."

"Yours?"

He wet his lips. Chains wasn't comfortable with emotion. He'd never been shown love or affection in the orphanages, and his adulthood was a mix of violence and distrust. But there was something special about Lori, and for the first time in his life, he had no desire for other women.

"Listen, I'm not going to kill or hurt you. I thought you'd have realized that by now." He released her arm, his fingers grazing her thigh as he pulled away. "Anything you want, I'll give it to you. Why isn't that enough?"

She shifted slightly to the side, looking at him. "You can't force someone to love you, Chains. Why would you want that?"

He frowned and stood up. "I never asked you to love me," he said. He began his climb up the stairs. Before he reached the top, he turned. "But don't be mistaken. You *are* mine."

\*\*\*\*

Lori watched the door close behind Chains. Part of her wanted to shout out for him to come back down. Even though she was used to being alone in life, being trapped in the basement with little social interaction was messing with her head. She needed to talk. Right now, she wanted to scream.

Her traitorous body lit up every time Chains visited her, to the point she swore she'd have a spontaneous orgasm. The man was built like a Greek god, all hard, lean muscle. His eyes, they held so much angst and darkness. She'd noticed it in the diner, but hadn't paid much attention to it. Now, all she had was time.

She wanted to hate him. She *should* hate him. The man was a murderer. The saddest part was, her kidnapper had been the nicest man she'd ever met. Her own father had been cold and selfish, her boss a prick, and every other man either abused her or treated her like trash. Chains was different. He made her feel like a princess … locked in a basement rather than a tower. And he'd killed … *for her*.

Lori looked around the basement. It was nicer than her apartment, that's for sure, professionally finished with only the best craftsmanship. She only had one leg shackle on now, and it was long enough for her to get around easily. There was everything she could want, and he never denied her a thing—except her freedom.

The first few days had been her honeymoon phase, all excitement and disbelief. It had been fun— takeout, long conversations, playful banter. Too good to be true. When she realized Chains had no plans on letting her leave, she began to panic. Who would help take care of her siblings? Yes, they were getting older, and they weren't her responsibility, but she cared too much. Now that she'd been returned to the basement, with too much time to think and process her life, she wasn't so sure what she wanted. Freedom would mean finding a new job, living on the streets since her rent wasn't paid last week, and dealing with the usual deep-seated loneliness that paralyzed her in depression many nights.

*Chains.* She knew nothing about him. Well, not enough. And besides his obsession with keeping her trapped in his house, she didn't know his intentions. He hadn't made a move on her and hadn't asked for anything. The strangest part—the man seemed genuinely attracted to her. Made her feel beautiful and special. She'd been fed so much bullshit since childhood about never finding a husband because she was too fat and awkward. Those toxic words had settled in deep, creating roots in her self-esteem. It felt indescribable to be wanted, cherished, and spoiled by this stranger. The longer she stayed, the more the real world became a distant blur. She felt so lonely, so forgotten. There was no one in the world who'd give a shit she'd disappeared from the world. Maybe she shouldn't be so eager to escape. There was nothing waiting for her beyond these walls.

She'd fallen asleep, and only woke to the sound of someone walking upstairs, and then a strip of light from under the door sent a soft glow of light down the stairs. Lori shifted amongst her blankets and hugged her pillow.

When she heard the locks on the door, she closed her eyes. He checked on her every night without fail, like a loving parent. Nobody had ever checked on her before. He'd just stand or sit near her for a while, then return to the main floor.

She pretended to sleep.

Tonight was no different, except he'd been gone for hours before she finally fell asleep. The complete silence had been unnerving.

His footsteps came closer, and her heartrate picked up, a mix of nerves, excitement, and a nagging desire. She heard the sound of the chair legs scraping the floor, then only his breathing. She'd almost think he'd left if not for the delicious scent of his musky cologne. She associated that smell with him alone, and it instantly brought down her anxiety.

He made a little sound, similar to a chuckle.

"I know you're awake," he finally said. His voice was deep and smooth. Not once had he lost his temper or made her feel scared by his words. It was her imagination driving her crazy.

Should she keep faking?

Chains sighed, picking up her leg chain that pooled on the floor by her bed. "When I was young, they used to chain me up and beat me shitless. I was weak back then, so I had no choice but to take it." More silence. "I keep telling myself this is different because your chains are to keep you safe." He dropped the metal to the floor.

Lori kept her eyes shut tight.

"I remember once when I was twelve, they broke at least four of my ribs. When they were done with me, I was on my own. No parents, no doctor, nobody but myself." He shifted in his seat. "There were others, of course. They beat this one girl right in front of me. I thought she was dead when they left. She made it through, but I still remember the black eye on her pretty face. I was too fucking scared to help her."

She may be a fool, but she pushed herself up into a sitting position. "You helped *me*," she said.

Lori wasn't sure why, but there was a connection between them. A weird, twisted connection that she couldn't understand. She was inexplicably drawn to him. Even though Chains was surrounded by darkness, there was a reason for it, triggers from deep in his past.

"When I saw you in the diner, your beautiful face

beaten, your eyes sad—I had to do something. Had to fix it. I've changed a lot in the past twenty years. I'll never be a victim, never stand on the sidelines, either."

She wanted to ask why he'd kidnapped her. He could have dealt with Carlton and not taken her home, chaining her in his basement. It didn't make sense. "Then why are you punishing me?"

He narrowed his eyes in confusion. "Punishing you? I'm trying my best to make you happy."

"You could have helped me without trapping me here."

His shoulders were back, his chin slightly jutted up. The man had a strong jaw and full lips. "I've done a lot of bad shit in my life, but I've been through a hell of a lot worse. I like to think of you as a bit of mercy thrown my way, and trust me there's never been much."

To hear that she was somehow a blessing to Chains was indescribable. From nothing to someone's everything? As much as she wanted this fantasy to be real, she had to think logically.

"What about me? My freedom?"

He licked his lips. "I'm not sure what the fuck I'm doing." Chains sat only a foot away. He leaned over and ran the backs of his fingers along her cheek. "Stay with me."

There was such vulnerability in his tone. Her own emotional response surprised her. Why did she care? Lori closed her eyes and savored his touch. In that moment, she realized how starved she was for affection. At twenty-five, she was a working machine, an empty, sad working machine. It was no way to live.

"Forever?" Part of her wanted him to say yes, but the other part was terrified he'd say no.

"Is that so bad?"

"You terrify me," she said.

"You don't look terrified."

She shook her head. "This kind of fear is different. I'm afraid of how you make me feel. I shouldn't want any of this."

"Stop listening to all those voices in your head," he said. "They don't know what they're talking about." He smiled at her, and she swore she fell in love just a bit.

"Do you want to come upstairs and take a shower?" he asked. Only then did she realize she was holding his forearm with both hands. She gasped and dropped her arms, tears instantly pooling in her eyes.

"I'm sorry." She felt so embarrassed. Lori was a mess, a needy, pathetic mess.

"It's okay, baby girl. I'm yours. Don't be shy with me."

He pulled a key from his pocket, and then squatted down to release her ankle bond. Chains rubbed the skin, even though he'd wrapped the anklet in soft fabric. She loved the feel of his rough hands on her skin. He forever moved slowly, deliberately. It was almost hypnotic. As he rose, he braced both hands on the mattress on either side of her. His shoulders were broad, his biceps bulging with toned muscle. She couldn't breathe, couldn't move. His face was so close to hers, his masculine signature enveloping her. She'd never craved anything more at that moment than his kiss. Maybe more.

Lori had never been intimate with a man. Considering the neighborhood she grew up in, she counted her virginity a triumph. There was no way she'd end up a baby-making machine like her mother. Chains had gotten under her skin. He was protective yet dangerous.

Chains brushed his lips against hers, slow and tender. "Dreams aren't all they're cracked up to be," he whispered. "You were right, Lori. You can't make someone love you."

Then he stood up, pulling away emotionally and physically. She wanted to scream for him to love her, to kiss her, anything. "I thought you weren't looking for love."

He held out his hand to help her up to her feet. She didn't hesitate.

## Chapter Five

Chains liked her ass. Watching her walk ahead of him, he admired the rounded curves that called for a man to grab hold of. Lori really was a dream, and for him, she was his prize.

"Turn left," he said.

"You can't keep me here forever."

He was growing tired of her thinking that there was a chance of her leaving. It wasn't going to happen. He'd even fight Boss for the right to keep her. Everything else he'd given up in life because there hadn't been anything worth keeping. When it came to Lori, she made him want to fight.

She was the first person he'd known that didn't make him want to kill, but to actually protect. All of his instincts wanted to guard her, and to keep her from harm.

Now *that* shit scared him.

Lori looked back at him. "Are you not going to answer me?"

"I don't know if I like you having a bit of sass or not." He moved his finger in a circle, telling her to turn back around. She did so with a huff, but he saw the spring in her step. Lori may not like it, but being with him, it had given her confidence, even though it had only been a week. They entered the main bedroom, and he waited as she admired the room once again. She seemed to really like his bedroom, which again satisfied him. He wanted to please her, to find everything that her heart wanted.

The truth was, he wanted her to want for nothing, and the only way to do that, was to give her everything.

"It's so big."

"I've heard that a lot of the time as well," he said, trying to ease the mood and crack a joke.

She looked over her shoulder at him. "I bet you say that to all of the women."

"Nope, just the ones I want to impress."

She crossed her arms, and turned toward him.

"I can show you if you want," he teased.

"No, that's fine. I just want the shower."

"Can I tempt you with a bath?" He brushed past her after shutting his bedroom door. Chains wondered if she'd make a run for it, but she didn't. She didn't even look toward the door, instead, following him as he picked up one of the many bath salts he'd purchased just for her.

"Are they laced with poison?" she asked.

He narrowed his eyes in insult. "No. They're designed to help you relax, to chill the fuck out. I'm not going to poison you." He stepped up close to her, running a finger down her neck, stroking over her pulse. "I have many ways I like to end people, and poison I consider to be quite dull."

She swallowed, but he also saw her eyes dilate.

Lori didn't fear him.

He liked that.

"You know this is weird, right? Buying women bath salts. You don't really know me."

"I know you've never been treated like anything other than a babysitter. I imagine this is the first week you've had a decent meal every night. I also imagine you've never had anyone to talk to who not only listens, but also understands."

She took a step back at that, and he noticed when he mentioned stuff about her, she always withdrew into herself. Almost as if she was afraid that he'd see too much. He saw her. He saw deep inside her soul, and what was more, he recognized it. She yearned for someone like him, even if it did scare her. That was okay.

He was going to take care of her, and show her

another life, one where she didn't get another person's baby thrown into her arms, and told to deal. From now on, she'd be priority number one, no one else.

"I like lavender," she whispered.

Reaching into the drawer, he pulled out three of the salts. "You can take as long as you want."

"You're not going to stay and watch?" she asked, as he made his way toward the door.

"We've only just met, Lori. I don't think you're ready for that." He winked.

Leaving the bathroom, he grabbed his cell phone, and quickly checked his emails. He had Maurice on tracking duty. He knew at least three of the six different identities that Xavier often used, and with those, he was able to track his movements all from the comfort of his own home.

Maurice had sent him a breakdown of all the purchases and stops that Xavier had made, and it wasn't all that impressive. A couple of motel stops, Italian and Mexican restaurant purchases. What he did find interesting was the bill for two. A woman? A job? Maurice attached the images that had been taken by cameras within the area, and he saw that Xavier had a different woman at each stop.

Interesting.

He didn't know what the big deal was with Xavier. Sure, he killed a load of people, and didn't have a soul—that wasn't new in his line of work. As far as he was concerned all Boss was doing was collecting killers like normal people collected trophies.

"Are you still there?" she asked.

He put his cell phone away, not bothering with Boss's email for now. He focused on the woman a few feet away in his bathroom.

"I'm still here so don't try to make a run for it."

"Pity because that's what I was planning. To run out of a house showing off my bare ass."

He smirked at her sarcasm. "You know I've got no problem spanking that ass." He could imagine her eye roll.

Now, if anyone else gave him that kind of sass, he'd have ended them long ago. She was different, and he wanted her.

His cock hardened just imagining her standing before him with her large tits thrust out, begging to be touched. He'd worship every single inch of her, and would do so every single day because that was what she deserved, and he'd be the one to give it to her.

It had been weeks now since he'd fucked a woman, which was a rarity for him. His life had always been a crazy mix of sex and killing. Now that Lori had entered the mix, she was all he could think about, leaving him with the worst case of blue balls.

Moving toward the door, he leaned against the frame, and stared in. She had enough bubbles in the water to hide her body from view. The scent of lavender was heavy in the air. He liked it. She'd pinned her hair on top of her head, and she smiled at him. She looked like a fucking angel.

"Do you even know how to spank?" she asked.

"You're really going to ask me that? I kill for a living."

She didn't know who she was fucking with. He was trying to be a gentleman, and she was baiting him as if he'd never played this game.

"Yeah, I don't think this is a good idea. I can't believe I'm even having a discussion with you right now. I forgot about what you've done."

"Carlton was an asshole who deserved to die. Don't forget that, sweetheart."

"Did he really? Do people really deserve to die?" she asked.

He smirked. "What about child abusers, rapists, and shit like that?"

She sighed. "I don't know. How can you? I mean, did you go to some kind of school to learn how to do it?"

Chains moved to take a seat on the toilet. It was the first time a woman had ever been interested in hearing about his life, and he was intrigued by her.

"My life wasn't a good one. Since I was a kid I've been taught how to use a gun, every kind of weapon, and of course, use these." He held up his hands. He'd killed a lot more people with his bare hands than he'd ever done with a weapon.

"I'm sorry."

"Why are you sorry?"

"I can't imagine you had a good childhood, and I find that incredibly sad. I feel yours was shattered even before it began."

He stared at her, seeing the sincerity in her gaze. Chains had witnessed a couple of men at Killer of Kings fall for different women. He'd often wondered what had made their women fall for them. He wasn't an expert, but he didn't imagine killers rated high on dating sites.

The whole risk of being killed ruined any chance of that. Hitmen learned early on that close relationships were a weakness to exploit. "You haven't had a good childhood either. You've done nothing but care for kids that aren't yours."

"They're still my brothers and sisters."

"Doesn't make it right."

"It doesn't make it wrong either," she said.

He smirked. "You're telling me that you've never thought about leaving? About having that once in a lifetime chance where you didn't have to change shitty diapers or worry about getting them to school, or even have to listen to another pregnancy announcement?" He saw the tears in her eyes. "It's not wrong to be selfish, Lori. It's your life as well, and you need to see that."

She sat up in the water, and stared at him. "You always make it sound so easy. Like it's not going to ruin everyone's life. I'm not like you. I can't be selfish."

Was he selfish for keeping her prisoner? He thought he was doing her a service, but what the fuck did he know?

He moved from his seat, kneeling on the tiles close to the tub. Resting his arms on the side of the bath, he stared at her, wishing that the bubbles would disperse and he'd get a nice view of those perky fat tits.

"Whose life are you going to ruin?" he asked. "I hate doing this as I hate seeing you upset, but there hasn't been a notice issued that you're missing."

"What?"

"I checked. I went by your place, and no one in your family has reported you missing." He saw the tears fill her eyes.

"They don't care?"

Chains gritted his teeth as anger began to flood his veins, his muscled tensing. He didn't want to see her cry, and certainly not for assholes. They didn't deserve her.

Reaching out, he swiped a tear off her cheek. "Don't cry for them."

"I'm … not loved. They don't care about me. I sacrificed everything for them."

She pressed her face against her hands, and Chains couldn't handle it anymore. Climbing into the bath, fully dressed, he pulled her into his arms. *He* wanted her. He cared, and Chains knew he'd do anything to make sure she'd be all right.

\*\*\*\*

Lori had known. Deep down she'd known that her parents didn't really care about her. They never asked her about her day, always speaking about their own problems. This just … hurt. She'd hoped that they'd miss her, but clearly, she'd just been another child in a long line of them. Lori felt small and alone, like a little girl craving her parents' love. But she was a woman now—a lonely, pathetic woman with nothing to her name.

Chains held her tightly, and even though she was naked, she welcomed his touch. Craved it. Needed it. She had no one else, which was really pathetic. This killer cared about her more than her own family did. He'd killed Carlton for hurting her. In the short time she'd been with him, even though she'd been chained in the basement, he'd taken excellent care of her. The time they shared, she actually relished those visits. She didn't want to lose his touch, not now, not ever. She was the star of some twisted fairy tale.

He stroked her hair, and she closed her eyes, resting her head against his sodden shirt.

"You're not alone," he said. The deep rumble of his voice calmed her.

"You don't know me."

"Then tell me everything. Show me who Lori is, and I'll tell you about myself."

"You'll want something though. Everyone always wants something."

She lifted her head up, and he offered her a smile. Why did she feel so comfortable with him? He'd admitted he killed and it was what he did for a living, but she felt comfortable with him. Safe.

"Don't leave. Don't try to run. That's all I ask."

"Really? Out of everything you could have or want, you just don't want me to run away?" she asked.

"No. I want you to give us both this chance. I won't hurt you. I won't even touch you. I just … I'd like to know you."

"No one cares who I am."

His palm cupped her cheek, the pad of his thumb rough against her skin as he stroked her skin. "I care. It's why I want you all to myself."

She rested her cheek against his touch, closing her eyes as she did so. "Yes."

"What?"

"I promise I won't run, but you've got to let me outside at least once. I promise I won't scream or beg for attention. We could just walk up and down the street."

"Why does going outside mean so much to you?" he asked.

"Because it's something I've always done. If Mom and Dad were fighting, I'd leave the tiny flat, and go sit on the swings near where we lived. If the smell was too much, sleeping outside wasn't a problem. It helped me think."

He sighed. "We'll go out after you've eaten something, and it's dark."

"Why do we have to go out in the dark?" she asked.

"I don't like the day very much, and to relax, there has to be at least a little darkness. In my life, shadows are a comfort."

"This is so strange. I guess you're the bogeyman, aren't you?"

"You're quite comfortable in my lap. Is that not strange to you?"

She stared at him, and he did the same right back at her. "We're both strange."

He winked at her. "Are you going to cry again?" he asked.

"No, I'm all cried out."

"I don't want to see you cry, not for them, not for anything. It hurts me." He rubbed at his chest, and she melted. Already he cared enough not to see her cry.

Chains climbed out of the tub first, grabbing a towel, which he held open in an offering. "Are you ready to come out, princess?"

She giggled, cautiously stepping up, and into the towel. Each little act that showed he cared filled her with such warmth. She was growing addicted to his touch, to the way he spoke and cared about her. Lori prayed it wasn't an elaborate act because she'd never been a great judge of character when it came to men.

He never raised his voice either. She appreciated that. It was a rest for her soul not having to walk on eggshells all the time.

He led her out into the bedroom. She found some clothes already waiting for her. "I'll have food ready downstairs."

She watched him leave, and knew instantly this was a test. If she tried to run for it, she'd go back to the basement, and wait until he built up some trust. She quickly got changed, and found herself across from a large mirror with an elaborate gold leaf frame. The clothes fit perfectly, and rather than making her look fat, they fit to every curve as if they'd been designed her for.

Looking into her own eyes at her reflection she seemed … happy. How weird was that? Alone with a man she barely knew who'd been taking care of her, and she was happy. None of this made any sense to her, and yet it did.

Rubbing her hands together, she took a deep breath. She didn't want to run. Even if she knew she could get away with it. The life he'd taken her from wasn't anything to covet. In fact, the life she'd led had been a fucking nightmare. Work, dealing with kids, and more work. Loneliness and sadness. She didn't want to go back to that life, and yes, she did also want to be a little bit selfish.

Chains made her feel so many things. Carlton had disgusted her, and she'd hated his touch. She never wanted any part of him or his lifestyle, and always fought to stay away from him. With Chains, it was different. She wished he'd take what he wanted, but he had the control of a saint. He always looked her up and down, but it felt like a caress, a brand of ownership. She wanted to belong … to him.

Her body felt alive when she was with him, and she liked to push, just a little, to see if he'd snap. He wouldn't snap. She knew it deep down in her core. Out of the entire world filled with women, Chains had picked her.

When everyone else overlooked her, and she'd been cast in shadow, feeling lost and alone—he'd noticed her.

Leaving the bedroom, she passed several windows, and even the main front door, and stepped into the kitchen. He stood, arms folded, leaning against the counter. Putting a hand on her hip, she winked at him.

"Thought I was going to run?"

"Any sane woman would have."

"I never claimed to be sane," she said.

He moved out of the way, and she saw some fresh cartons of Chinese food. She sat on a stool and picked up the chopsticks to eat.

For several seconds, he watched her eat, before doing the same.

"I like watching you eat," he said.

"That's not weird at all." She took another slurp of noodles. "I think I've eaten more in the past week than

I ever have before. You wouldn't think that for looking at me though." She ran a hand down her backside. She'd always been a big girl with fuller curves. It didn't matter how much she tried to diet. By diet, she meant starve herself. Being part of a poor family, she didn't exactly have money to waste on fancy diet plans. She swore she gained weight by air alone.

Eating no food was simply a cheaper alternative.

"You'll never go without food again."

"You know what it was like to go without anything?" she asked.

"Yes."

"Sucks, doesn't it? Did you have any parents?"

"No parents. I was in the system, or what people tried to claim was the system. Far from here."

"Oh, at least I had parents … I guess. Whenever I'd go to them to ask about getting food, they'd always need cigarettes or beer. Mom would constantly be spending money on new clothes, and she always said it was her money, and we should just be grateful that we had a roof over our heads."

"You never should have given your money to them," Chains said. "I'm surprised you didn't tell them to fuck off once you turned eighteen."

"I tried to help out. I thought I was doing the right thing, and it was all wrong. I was just helping them spend more money on themselves."

Her appetite was gone, so she put the food back on the counter, and shoved her hands into her pockets. "I can be a real downer at times, huh?"

Chains chuckled. "I've never been called the life of the party."

She didn't know why she found his words so funny but she did, and held her stomach as they both shared the laughter together. He looked past her shoulder, outside. "Would you care to go for a walk with me?"

"I'd love to."

He offered her his arm, which she took. Chains opened the front door, and as she crossed the threshold, she found herself gasping, almost believing leaving the house wasn't possible.

Once he locked the house, she held onto him tightly, not wanting to let him go. His arms were thick and hard with muscle. It was in that moment that she realized she didn't want to run from him. The short time she'd been with Chains, he'd made her feel so much happiness that the thought of not seeing him again filled her with dread.

They walked away from the house, and for a good ten minutes neither of them spoke. She loved the feel of the cool breeze on her skin, and the freshness in the air. Everything felt surreal, and amazing. Like the first day of forever.

Opening her eyes, she spotted a park, and quickly urged him over toward it. With it being so late, there wasn't anyone around, and she made him take a seat in a swing.

"What are you doing?"

"I'm going to push you." She pressed against his back, and she saw he wasn't having fun. "Come on, Chains, don't be a drag. We can have a lot of fun together if you just let it happen." She pushed his back again, and this time, he didn't fight against her.

He lifted his legs in the air, and she giggled as she pushed his back again. Together they could have the happiness she'd always dreamed of having.

## Chapter Six

On the walk back home, Chains checked his phone. Almost immediately after, his mood was off. The neighborhood was dark, only the rare streetlight giving them some light.

"Is everything okay?" she asked.

He nodded. "Look, I need to go out for a bit. Shouldn't take too long. I didn't want to do this, but do you mind waiting downstairs?"

"You still don't trust me." It wasn't a question, but a fact. She wasn't sure if she should feel insulted or not after the progress they'd made.

They walked up the front stairs of his house. The front light was off, so it was all shadows. He stopped in front of the door, his keys in hand. "It's not that. I'm just being cautious. I can't risk losing you."

It had only been a week, but Lori hoped that he'd trust her one day. She wasn't angry, though, because she sensed this was about his insecurity, not a control thing. They were very much alike. Lori didn't mind humoring him because the alternative was her old life—one she wanted no part of.

"Fine."

She wanted to ask where he was going, but she suspected she wouldn't like the answer, so kept her mouth shut. He led her back into the basement once they were inside. It felt like her own personal space. Chains made sure she had every comfort possible, so it was almost a relief to return to the basement.

He pressed his hand against the wall near her head, their bodies close. "Did you like your walk?"

She nodded. The truth was his closeness affected her. Lori ached for him to kiss her, touch her, claim her. It was one thing to make her feel wanted and special, but she needed more.

"You're quiet."

Lori nibbled her lower lip. The faint scent of his cologne was driving her crazy. What kind of man kept a woman prisoner and never made a move? She wasn't even sure he liked her in a romantic way. Everything about him was an enigma. "Just thinking."

"About what?"

"What am I doing here? I mean, what're your intentions with me?"

His eyes were so dark, impossible to read. "I haven't thought that far ahead."

Lori had never been with a man sexually, so she didn't want to push too far and regret the decision. She'd just never been wanted by a man, never felt desirable. Her self-esteem had always been in the dumps thanks to her weight, and the neglect at home.

"Am I supposed to be your prisoner, or have you decided to skip the dating and steal yourself a wife?" Lori held her breath. She'd put out a feeler, hoping to learn more of how he felt about her. Her worst fear was finding out he had no sexual interest in her. Maybe he'd even laugh at the suggestion.

"I never planned on any of this. When I saw you in the diner, everything changed for me," he said. "I was satisfied fucking random women, living alone with only my job to keep me focused. Then, in the blink of an eye, it wasn't enough. You're all that matters to me now."

"What does that mean?"

He narrowed his eyes, obviously not catching her drift. "It means you're the only woman I want, Lori." Chains ran the backs of his fingers along her jawline, and she closed her eyes, leaning into his touch.

"Chains…"

He kissed her on the mouth, his tongue

demanding entrance. Every bone in her body felt like jelly the moment his lips met hers. She reached up and held his shoulders, kissing back, savoring the intimacy. He moved lower, suckling her pulse point, then kissing down her neck. His rough stubble scraped her skin, but she loved his big body weighing down over her. Her breathing picked up, her entire body thrumming with a need she'd never known. When he ran his hand down her side, he growled once he reached her hip, his fingers squeezing hard into her flesh. She gasped, and he abruptly pulled away, putting more than an arm's length between them.

"I'm sorry," he said, running a hand over his shaved head. "I have to be careful with you."

"Why?" she blurted the word, missing their connection. Lori wanted to understand. Had she done something wrong?

"I'm trying to take things nice and slow. I'm not used to being a gentleman, but I know you're a virgin, Lori."

Her mouth fell open, and she knew her cheeks were turning red. How could he know that? She wanted to refute him, but it was the truth. "Don't you want me?"

"Stop tempting me. You're playing a dangerous game, sweetheart." He cupped her face with both hands, then kissed her forehead with a chaste kiss. "I'll check on you when I get back. Don't wait up."

Then he was gone, heading up the stairs before locking the basement door. What the hell had just happened? At least she couldn't accuse the man of using her for sex. She couldn't get the man in her bed if she tried.

She looked down at herself, remembering the path his hands had taken. Lori closed her eyes and savored the memory. Her pussy throbbed, her heart still racing.

Lori walked over to her bed and flopped down on her back, staring blankly at the ceiling. Her imagination was on overdrive, and she yearned for that day, the day he'd strip her of her virginity. She'd gladly hand it over to Chains.

The hours passed, and he still hadn't returned. She'd read a few chapters in one of her books, but couldn't get into the novel, not with her mind elsewhere. When she heard footsteps upstairs, her heart jumped. Lori sat up on the bed and rushed to the mirror to check her hair. She wanted to look good for Chains, to be the only woman he ever wanted.

It was a relief knowing he was home. Every time he left could be the last. He killed people, which meant he could be on the receiving end one day. The thought of losing him filled her with dread.

Why wasn't he coming downstairs?

Lori waited, pacing the basement. She heard him going up and down the stairs to the second level, and doors and cupboards were opening and closing. Something had to be wrong.

When he began to rattle the doorknob to the basement, she began to worry. Chains had the keys, so why was he trying to break in? When he began to kick in the basement door, over and over until the hinges splintered off, she rushed to the far end of the basement and crouched down low.

The footsteps coming down the steps were ominous, slow, and measured.

She peeked from her hiding spot. It wasn't Chains. The realization sent adrenaline racing through her veins. This guy had black, shoulder-length hair. He ran a hand through it as he assessed the space. A tattoo creeped up his neck. This was probably some murderer looking for Chains. And she was going to be collateral damage.

Her life flashed before her eyes. What a pathetic existence she'd had. Struggling, suffering, going without. Never loved. As all her trials filled her mind, she still didn't want to die. Chains had opened her eyes to something new and wonderful.

The stranger rooted around her stuff, tossing her clothes from the drawers. Then he spotted her. He whipped his head around and pulled out a handgun, aiming it at her.

She froze, unable to move or breathe.

"Who are you?" he asked, stalking forward.

"Lori," she whispered.

"Are you Chains's woman? Tell me the fucking truth or I'll kill you."

She'd never been so scared. Lori shook her head. "I'm his prisoner."

The harsh lines on the man's face vanished, and a smirk appeared on his face. "I knew he was a sick fuck, but come on!" He laughed and put his gun back in the holster.

He came closer and squatted down in front of her. His eyes were dark, and he had several scars on his cheek.

"Please don't hurt me."

"You're worried about me? You should be happy I showed up when I did. Keeping a woman prisoner in his basement? I thought I was twisted, but Chains just took the prize." He stood up and held out his hand. "Today's your lucky day."

She did as told, terrified of what he was capable of. He hoisted her to her feet and pointed to the stairs. She kept looking back at him as she walked up to the main level, worried he'd shoot her in the back.

"Where are you taking me?"

"Sorry, but I don't run a taxi service. I'll set you free, but then you're on your own." Before they went through the busted doorway, he pulled out his gun again, looking in every direction as they walked through the hallway. "Keep moving," he said. "This fucker's been playing with me, and I want to know why."

He kept talking out loud. His rambling made her feel better because silence would be worse. When they reached the front door, he grabbed the back of her shirt, directing her forward like a shield. He directed her to keep walking up the road until they reached a dark alleyway.

Where was Chains?

She was glad he wasn't home because he could have been killed.

The jangle of keys was followed by a car in the alley turning on, the headlights illuminating the area. He made his way to the driver's side door, leaving her at the edge of the alley.

"Now what?" she asked.

"You're on your own, baby. If you were smart, you'd get far away from that fucking psycho." Then he got in his car and burned rubber getting to the main street, leaving her in his exhaust. She stood in the same spot for the longest time, the sound of dripping and an empty bottle toppling sending a shiver of unease up her spine.

She wasn't sure what she should do next. Go home? Find her way back to Chains's basement? Now that she had her freedom, her thoughts cleared. Maybe she had Stockholm Syndrome, and Chains was nothing like she'd made him out to be. This was her chance to be free, outside, no rules but her own.

Tears began to fill her eyes. She didn't want to

make a choice, wasn't sure what she should feel. Lori was a damn mess.

****

Chains wanted to spend his time with Lori playing house, but he was still on the payroll at Killer of Kings. Boss liked him to be his driver whenever there could be trouble. He knew Chains could handle anything if shit went down. Tonight, Boss wanted to send a personal warning to a new family moving in on the city. They'd been going after a lot of the same contracts, which was fine, but when they tried to get in the way of Boss's men, the game changed. After Boss said his piece, Chains needed to send a message to their crew. At least one of them would be sporting a body bag tonight.

Killing was no harder than breathing to Chains. He'd been doing it since puberty, so it was natural … nothing personal. People asked him if he ever felt sorry for his victims or their families, but in truth, he didn't. He wasn't sure what the fuck that meant, but he preferred not to think about it. The orphanage, and later the streets, in Russia had made him what he is today, so he refused to take blame for the monster he'd become.

"About time." Boss got in the back of Chain's car. "You have the address I sent?"

"We'll be there in twenty-five minutes."

Boss leaned back against the custom leather seats. Since Chains did most of Boss's driving these days, he'd been set up with the very best. "This shouldn't take long. I have a date tonight, so I don't plan on humoring these assholes."

"Anything serious?"

Boss scoffed. "As serious as pussy can be."

Chains didn't say anything. Only a couple weeks ago he felt the exact same way. He'd fuck different bitches every night. He didn't want to know their names or see them more than once.

Then came Lori.

All he could think about was the softness of her lips and gentle touch of her hands. She was nothing like the women he'd been with. Lori was pure innocence, damaged and vulnerable. The only pussy he could think about was the sweet virgin one locked up in his basement. And he didn't mind waiting.

He'd planned to get more domestic, keep her with him in his bedroom at night. But this gig with Boss threw a wrench in his plans, and he couldn't risk her running off. Because then he'd have to chase. She was his, and he wouldn't let her go.

The city lights cast out the darkness until they hit the suburbs. They pulled up to the address, but Chains went around back, parking on the street. The entire time he'd taken in the area to memory. His body was fully strapped, and his trunk had a small arsenal. Boss always had men from Killer of Kings on speed dial. If shit went ugly, Viper, Bain, or Killian would be on top of things in a hurry. There were dozens of other men on Boss's payroll, depending on the area.

He shut off the engine. "You have a contact?" he asked.

"You know how much I like to show up unexpected," said Boss. The asshole lived for the kill. Chains didn't need to ask if he was packing heat. The man was born ready.

Chains exited the vehicle, looking up and down the street. He reached inside his black leather jacket, feeling the handles of all his guns. Boss had custom holsters made for him, so Chains was a one-man army, and skilled with every kind of weapon. He didn't care how many fuckers he was numbered against because he was confident in his ability to clear a room.

They walked across the street and then up the sidewalk, Boss a few feet behind him. The man was his boss, but Chains trusted and respected him. He'd helped him make a new life far from his miserable homeland. And he knew Boss had a soft spot for him, even if he didn't say it out loud.

"This the place?" he asked, not turning around.

"Keep going. It's eleven o'clock, so they'll be playing cards in the guest house."

Chains kept walking, keeping on guard. As Boss said, the windows of the guesthouse out back were warm with light. The neighborhood was dark and remote, not much outdoor lighting at the side of the house.

His adrenaline started to kick in after they hopped the low iron fence. It had been a while since he'd been on a job with Boss. The last man he'd killed had been a quick contract that he handled in less than an hour.

Boss waited safely on the periphery while Chains kicked in the door. There were six men at a round table, three on a sofa, and two standing near a small bar.

He pulled out two Glocks, aiming them in outstretched arms. "No one fucking move."

Of course, some of them didn't seem to understand the simple instructions. They probably had huge balls considering it was eleven to one. Chains popped the kneecaps of the two guys reaching for their handguns, and nailed another in the hand. Everything happened so fast, they didn't have time to process the invasion.

"Don't think about it," he said to the fat guy on the couch. When he had their attention, Boss strolled in the room. One of the men at the table must have recognized the infamous Killer of Kings founder and stood up, his chair scraping the tiles. Chains shot him between the eyes. His body crashed down, and the table tipped with him, cards and chips scattering.

"Excuse the intrusion," said Boss, stepping over the mess. "It's come to my attention you're giving my men a hard time. That doesn't sit well with me. If you're not aware that I own this fucking city, then let this be your wake-up call. I'm good at minding my own business, but when you step on my toes, that's when we have a problem." Boss directed his attention to the older man at the table, so Chains assumed that was their ringleader. He was smoking a cigar, holding it in his fingers now that the table was overturned along with his ashtray. "Someone upright the fucking table."

The other men moved to put it back into place, ignoring the body on the floor. Boss pulled up a chair and sat down, knowing full well Chains had his back. He pulled out a wicked looking blade and began spinning it on its tip.

"You're messing with the wrong family," said the leader. He took a puff of his cigar, slowly releasing a cloud of white smoke.

Boss chuckled. "Try it on someone else."

"How many men do you have? We have men all over city. If anything happens to me, they'll want revenge."

"I know where every single one of your men live, where their families live, where their kids go to school. I know your mother's nurse, Mary Vazquez, makes sure she has warm milk before bed every night. It's a nice nursing home, by the way. With one phone call, I guarantee there would be no one left but you within the hour."

Chains winked when the asshole looked over at him. Boss wasn't playing either. Chains had seen him keep his promises on more than one occasion. The man didn't have a fucking conscience.

"I don't want any trouble," said the leader.

"Good to hear. I'd hate to have to get involved. Friends are always better than enemies." Boss stood up, pocketing his knife, and left the guest house.

Chains stayed behind, closing the door once Boss was gone. He smiled as the men looked at him with a mix of confusion. They always went for the right-hand men because it weakened the kingpin.

"Nothing personal. Just business, eh?" Chains shot the two men on either side of the leader, one in the heart, the other in the head, leaving zero chance of survival.

Once they were back in the car, Chains didn't waste any time getting out of the area. He took the highway, eager to drop Boss back at home so he could release Lori from the basement. She'd been fucking with his head, making it hard to focus on work.

"Any progress on El Diablo?" asked Boss, absently. Chains could see the light from his cellphone in the back.

"It won't take long. I've already mapped out his routine."

"Good. Good to hear. Once that's cleared up, I'll have a contract for you."

Tonight was just a maintenance call. A contract would be more involved, probably include tracking, intel, and death by a specified manner. Chains enjoyed the challenge, but also didn't want something that would take him far from home.

"Local?" he asked.

"Does it matter?" asked Boss. The old bastard had unparalleled intuition. Chains should have kept his mouth shut.

"Just asking."

Once he pulled up at Boss's mansion just outside

the city, he got out to open Boss's door. The old bastard had an evil gleam in his eye as he stood up. "Looks like you have an intruder on the home-front."

Chains whipped out his cellphone. His alarm system hadn't triggered.

"I have eyes on all my men. Can never be too safe."

"Who is it?" asked Chains. There was no way Boss didn't know what the fuck was going down.

"Like I said, I have a date. Handle your own shit."

Chains rushed around to the driver's side, biting his tongue to keep from telling Boss to *fuck off.* All he could think about was Lori locked in his basement. If anyone put one hand on her, he'd bring a firestorm of pain to the asshole. He sped down the highway toward his house, his heart racing. Material things could be replaced; Lori couldn't. He only hoped they didn't check the basement.

As he raced through the darkness, he realized that the little good left in him was tied to that girl. He wasn't just rushing to save her, but himself. Lori represented so much. She was his chance at redemption.

If anything happened to her, he'd become pure darkness.

## Chapter Seven

For the longest time Lori stood in the alleyway listening to the sounds all around her. The tears fell down her cheeks, and no matter how many times she wiped them away more kept coming. Any sane person would be happy to be free.

She'd been kidnapped, taken against her will, and she was so sad because she didn't want to go home. The thought of being just another babysitter tore her up. Her parents didn't love her, and in the past few days with Chains she'd felt … cared for.

Love was too strong a word for her to think or to feel. She wanted it for a long time, but she doubted that she'd ever have anyone love her. Rubbing her arms, she glanced around, realizing how dangerous it actually was being alone in an alleyway at this hour. She didn't have a clue where she was, or what the hell she was doing. After getting out of the alleyway, she began to walk in the direction that she'd been taken from. The next time she saw that man—and she couldn't for the life of her remember if he'd even given his name, it didn't matter—she was going to kick him where it hurt the most.

She hated this.

*Keep walking, Lori.*

The thought of going back home filled her with a sickness that she couldn't describe, something soul-deep.

*You used to walk the streets on your own.*

*Nothing has changed.*

*You're just used to a man caring now.*

The thought of Chains and his touch made her ache. She didn't want to leave him. Just the thought of never seeing him again or not experiencing his touch filled her with regret.

She stepped up the pace, wanting to get back the

way she'd come.

Panic filled her.

What if Chains thought she didn't want to be with him, or that she'd escaped of her own accord?

She loved her spot in the basement as stupid as that sounded.

It was the one space that no one could take from her.

He'd treated her with such tenderness, and she didn't want to lose that.

Wiping the tears from her cheeks, she moved with determination. In the strange man's haste to get her out of the house, she'd not even looked at the house where she'd come from.

"Please," she said, praying that Chains was home.

She ran around the corner when she collided with a hard, muscular chest. If strong arms hadn't caught her she'd have fallen to the floor.

Glancing up, she saw it was Chains, and she threw caution to the wind, wrapping her arms around his neck, and holding him tightly.

"You're here. You came back."

He held her in a firm embrace, and the heat of his hands made her feel safe.

"What happened?" he asked.

She didn't like how hard and cold he sounded. Like a business transaction.

"S-someone came in. I don't know his name. Something about you following him? Tailing him? I can't really remember. He asked if I was your woman and he aimed a gun at me." She pressed a finger to her forehead. "I thought he was going to kill me, Chains. Oh my God! I could have been dead by now."

"I would never let that happen, or let anyone ever hurt you," he said.

She stared into his eyes as his palm cupped her cheek.

Resting her head against his chest, she held onto him, never wanting to let him go.

"Hush, I've got you now."

"He just took me out, and then he left me in a dark alley."

"You didn't go home."

"I don't want to go home, Chains. I … I don't have a home. Not really. I don't have anyone who loves me or who cares." She pulled away, but he wouldn't let her go far.

Chains captured her chin, and forced her to look at him. "I care. Okay? I don't give a fuck about your family. They don't care about you, and they don't deserve you. You're mine, and I'm not ever letting you go."

His words should fill her with fear or panic. They didn't. She felt thrilled, and the smile on her lips was real. "Really?"

"Really." He ran his thumb across her lip. "Come on. Let's go see what the bastard took."

She followed Chains back to his home.

"Stupid fucking security."

"Are we staying here?"

"Nope. Because of El Diablo, we're heading up to my cabin, which even Boss doesn't know about." Chains closed the door behind him, and she followed along as he packed their cases with enough clothes to last a couple of weeks, by the looks of it.

Her hands were shaking, and she expected him to be angry at her. He seemed so calm. It's one of the things she liked about him—his control, his patience with her.

"I didn't want to go," she said, reaching out to grab his arm.

Chains stared at her. "Why didn't you tell him to stop?"

"I was scared. I don't really know what happened. One moment I was waiting for you, the next he was in the basement searching for something. What did you have down there?" she asked.

Chains smirked, but it was anything but friendly. "My boss has him on a goose chase right now. It would have been nice to know he planted a clue in my fucking house."

Lori frowned at him. "I don't know what you're talking about right now, and you keep talking to me as if I do."

He smiled. "One day, I'll tell you."

When he made to pass, she grabbed his arm, and hugged him. Closing her eyes, she breathed in his masculine scent, and just relaxed. He was her safety net.

For several seconds he didn't do a single thing. He simply held still and waited.

"Hold me," she said.

His hands went to her back. "What's wrong?" he asked.

"Nothing. Absolutely nothing. I'm just feeling … so much right now."

"Why?"

She exhaled a heavy breath. "I didn't want to go home. I just wanted to come back here to you." She eased back long enough to look at him. "And being here with you, I feel so alive." She cupped his cheek. "Is that weird?"

"I don't know. I've never been normal in my life."

"I'm starting to think normal is overrated, but I don't want to go back to my old life. Please, Chains, don't make me go back."

"I'm not going to make you go back." He covered her hand with his own.

Whenever he touched her, she got a thrill, and she didn't want to lose that.

"Kiss me."

Chains stared at her for the longest time. All she wanted was his lips on hers, and when he made no move to do that, she lost her patience with him. Gripping the back of his neck, she pulled his head down.

He could have fought her. He didn't.

His lips met hers, and everything that felt wrong in her world went away. The only person she wanted or cared about was right in front of her.

She traced her tongue across his lips, and when he opened, she plunged inside, deepening the kiss. Releasing a moan, she closed her eyes, and gave herself over to the pleasure of his lips. One of his hands held onto her head, and he sank his fingers into her hair. When he held her tightly, she melted against him, not wanting to let him go.

He broke away from the kiss and began to trail his lips down her neck.

Her nipples grew tight and her pussy slick. She wanted him so desperately.

Suddenly, he pulled away. "Not here."

"Why not?"

"It's not safe."

She tilted her head to the side, surprised that he'd stopped. "Wherever you are, it's safe."

Chains smiled. "Well … listen to me. I know what's good for the both of us, and staying here, is not good."

He grabbed both of their bags, and he took them downstairs toward the door, as she followed him out to the waiting car. Once the bags were inside the trunk, he opened the passenger door for her. She waited as he secured her seatbelt.

"I can do that," she said, trying not to laugh.

"I know you can, but I want to do it."

She felt warmth fill her as his hand brushed across her breasts. Pushing some of her hair off her face, she sat back waiting for him to climb into the car.

*He wants to take care of me.*

Chains got behind the wheel, and she waited for him to start the engine.

He didn't pull away from the curb though. They stayed still, and for several seconds she did nothing but wait.

Glancing around her, she then looked at him, and he looked torn.

"What is it?"

"I'm … thinking."

"You can't think and drive?"

He turned toward her. His gaze hard. "My cabin is a safe place." It sounded like he was thinking out loud. The interior lights clicked off, and the quiet was deafening.

"Safe like your house?" she asked.

"No. It's more secure than this."

"Then what's the problem?"

He stared straight ahead, his jaw twitching. "You're going to hate me."

"I don't get this, Chains. Don't you want to go to your safe house?" she asked.

He let out a heavy breath. "I'm going to regret this."

Chains suddenly grabbed her head and his other hand covered her face. There was a cloth in his hand, and she gasped, struggling against him.

"I'm sorry, baby, but I can't risk your safety.

You'll never know the way to the cabin. It's only me, and I will always take care of you."

Everything started to get blurry, and she stared into his eyes. She felt safe.

Even though he was putting her to sleep, just staring into his depths, she knew without a doubt that he was going to take care of her.

**\*\*\*\***

Chains parked outside of his cabin and took a deep breath of country air. The drive had been quiet with Lori passed out. After checking over his security on his cell phone, he'd seen El Diablo enter, and take the files Boss stashed away to blackmail El Diablo. Seeing how easily Boss was luring the other man into the Killer of Kings' web was really quite something. It just went to show that Boss was indeed the master at this game of cat and mouse.

Regardless of how Chains liked to watch this game, he still didn't like that it involved his home. He wanted to kill the bastard for pointing a gun at his woman, but El Diablo hadn't hurt her.

Climbing out of the car, Chains moved toward Lori, and stared down at her. Her eyes were closed, and she looked completely at peace with life. She was so beautiful, so sweet, and he absolutely adored her.

"I'm so sorry, baby." No one knew about his cabin. He kept the details separate from his life, and he rarely came here unless he felt a need to get away.

Lifting her up, he carried her from the car into his cabin, which was spotless.

He didn't linger, going straight to the bedroom, and placing her on the crisp sheets. "I'm going to take care of you for the rest of our life together."

Chains made sure she was tucked in nice and tight before heading back to grab their bags. From there, he closed the door, and locked it. Resting his head against the wood, he breathed a sigh of relief.

For the next week, he intended to be completely away from the world. No stress. No cell phones. No internet. No Boss.

Maurice would be tracking him, and if the man found anything, there would be an alert on his pager.

Stepping away from the door, he grabbed their bags, and set about putting their clothes in the closet. Every now and then, he glanced over at her, and watched her. He couldn't sleep right now. He was far too wired.

Once their clothes were away, he made his way into the sitting room. Grabbing one of the crime books from the shelves, he took a seat in his favorite chair, and sat back. He rarely allowed himself the pleasure of relaxing. Even in his home that El Diablo had just broken into, he knew anyone could find him. Boss knew where he lived, as did most of the Killer of Kings. Most of the time, he didn't mind it. He had this cabin that no one knew of, and that was the way he liked it.

Boss's incessant need, like some kind of father, to always know what they were doing, pissed him off. The only reason he'd put Lori to sleep for the journey was so that Boss couldn't interrogate her or use her to find this place.

This would be *their* place.

Time passed, and still sleep wouldn't come. He saw the sun coming up, so he headed to the kitchen and began to whip up some bacon and eggs.

The concoction he'd given her wasn't strong. She'd just had an extended night's sleep.

He heard her gasp at exactly six-thirty in the morning.

"You drugged me!"

Chains smiled. She sounded so outraged. It was

so cute. When she came into the kitchen, he held a plate of food like a shield. Her hair was all over the place, and she ran a hand down her face. She glanced at him then at the food, then at him again. "What the hell?"

"First, I did it for your own protection."

"Bullshit."

"It's not. The man I work for … he has ways and means of finding out whatever he wants. This place is the only thing I have. I don't want him to know about it, and I know Boss. He'll want to know where I go when he can't find me."

She frowned looking at him. "Boss? I can't … not right now. I'm hungry, and I'm pissed at you. I'm hungry even more though."

"I made you breakfast."

"Is it poisoned?"

"What's with you and poison? It's perfectly safe." He stole a piece of bacon from her plate. She watched him eat it, and when he made to take another piece she slapped his hand away.

"That's mine."

"In case you were worried that I was going to poison you."

She glared at him. "You already ate one piece. I want the food for myself. I've had a very trying experience tonight." She looked at the early morning light coming in the window. "Yesterday. I don't even know."

He chuckled.

Grabbing his own plate, he sat down at the table. He watched as Lori took another bite and moaned.

"I can't believe how hungry I am right now."

"You missed dinner last night."

Her gaze was still glaring. "Yeah, I know. You see, this guy nearly shot me."

"He didn't shoot you."

"Yeah, but what if he had?" she asked.

Chains gritted his teeth. "No."

"What do you mean, no?"

"I … can't think about it."

"You can't think about the thought of someone shooting me?"

"I wouldn't let it happen."

"You weren't there, Chains." She picked up her bacon with her fingers. "Yum, you know the only way to make this better would be if it was completely smothered in maple syrup."

He chuckled. "I'll remember that for next time."

"So … how would you have stopped him?" she asked.

Chains stared at her. He couldn't bring himself to even think about that. "I'd have killed the bastard if he hurt you. The fact that he pointed a gun at you. No. I can't do this."

She licked her lips, and stared at him. "He didn't shoot me."

"And when I see him, I'm going to make sure he pays for threatening you."

Neither of them spoke, and he stared at her. He couldn't do this.

He watched as she picked up her fork. She began to eat her eggs, and he watched her. "I'm not dead."

"No, you're not."

She ate another spoonful of eggs. "These are so tasty."

He didn't say anything and waited.

"The man … El something."

"El Diablo."

"Yes, when you see him again, I want be prepared," she said.

"What do you mean?" he asked.

"I don't want to be a victim or risk being hurt like that again. I want to be able to take care of myself, and I know the only way to do that is with you." She nibbled her lip and looked so cute.

"You want me to teach you about self-defense?"

"Yes. Maybe then I could stop you from drugging me again."

"I did it for your own good."

She snorted. "Right."

"Believe me or not, but if you ever meet Boss, and I bet you probably will, you'll see what I mean."

She finished her breakfast, and he handed her a cup of coffee. Once that was done, she offered to do the dishes and he watched her. It was somewhat surreal to feel like domestic bliss. She stood at the sink, and he watched her lift one leg up and scratch the back of her calf. Her rounded ass seemed to call to him, and he couldn't take his gaze away from her, not that he wanted to.

Lori was far too intriguing to watch. She had a fire inside her that he liked.

She finished the dishes, stacking them up with the rest of them in the kitchen. She wiped her hands on a towel resting against the sink.

"This is lovely." She looked around her.

"Take your clothes off," he said.

She paused and looked at him. "What?"

"You heard me, baby. I want you to strip for me."

"And if I don't want to?"

"Do you not want to get naked for me? It's just you and me here. No one else."

He saw her nipples tighten, and her breathing deepened. Color was high in her cheeks, and she looked ready to fuck.

Her fingers drummed against the counter, and he rested his head in his hand, watching her. His cock was already hard.

She grabbed her shirt and pulled it over her head revealing a white lace bra. Next, she wriggled out of her sweatpants.

White lacy underwear was all she stood in.

"Beautiful but that's not naked."

"No. It's not," she said, agreeing. She took a deep breath and began to remove the rest of her clothes.

Seconds later she stood in his kitchen, completely naked, and she looked nervous. To him though, she looked utterly breathtaking.

He couldn't believe how lucky he'd gotten, but there was no chance in hell that he was ever going to give her back. She belonged to him now.

All of his life he'd had things taken from him, and he wasn't going to allow that to happen again. Standing up, he didn't move closer. Pulling his shirt from his body, he threw it to the ground. Pushing his pants down, he heard her gasp as his cock sprang forward.

"Wow," she said.

"You like what you see?"

"What's not to like? You're all … hard and wow."

"And it's all for you." He liked having her gaze on him. Wrapping his fingers around his length he worked it from the tip down to the base then up again. The head was already leaking pre-cum.

He watched her as she stared at him. "This is how hard you make me."

"That's me?"

"Yes. This is all you. There's no one else in the world that I want. No woman could ever match you."

He sat down on the chair, and released his cock.

"Come here."

"If I come there you're going to touch me."

"Yes. You're going to like me touching you. I promise." He waited.

He would never force her. Chains had excellent control.

All she had to do was tell him to stop and he would. He saw the need in her eyes, though. She wanted this, and he wanted to give it to her.

Lori took a step forward then another. Within a few more steps she stood right in front of him. Her hands were clenched at her sides.

"Do you want me to touch you?" he asked.

"Yes, I want you to touch me."

"Are you afraid?" He tilted his head to the side. "And don't lie."

"I'm afraid of what I want, but I'm not afraid of you. I'm … when I'm with you I feel safe, and I don't want to lose that."

He reached out taking her hand. "I'll always take care of you, and I'll always give you what you need."

## Chapter Eight

Lori knew what she needed, and her own filthy thoughts shocked her. She was naked, vulnerable, and for the first time in her life, she didn't feel ashamed of herself. It was the way he looked at her.

With hunger.

He must have reflected her own desires. Chains had the body of a god, and she couldn't stop staring at all those hard, ripped muscles. He looked like a centurion from one of the movies she'd seen on Netflix, but this one was all hers. His cock was big and thick, and she couldn't imagine it even fitting inside her. Yet her lust outweighed her fears. If any man was to strip her of her virginity, she wanted it to be Chains. He'd put her first, showing her what she'd been blind to. Made her feel valuable. Safe. Desired.

"Has another man touched you, Lori?"

She shook her head. It wasn't a lie. Between working at the diner and babysitting, she had no time to socialize—not that any man showed interest in her. Catcalls and crude propositions at the bus stop at night didn't count.

"I like that," he said. "I've been holding back. It was important to me that you knew this wasn't about sex."

Lori bit her lip. "And now?"

"I'm not going anywhere, baby. So there's no sense in torturing myself anymore, is there?"

She needed him, had for a while now. His holding back had given her a complex and made her desperate for his touch. "No. I don't want you to hold back."

He was a lot taller than she was, all sinewy muscle. She dared to reach up and trace her fingers along his defined pecs, and then down his ripped abs. He had a lot of old scars, but one thing she noticed was the complete lack of tattoos.

Chains didn't move, allowing her to explore his body. When she reached low enough, he grabbed her wrist. She looked up to gauge his reaction. He licked lips. "Keep going, baby girl."

She swallowed her fears and wrapped her fingers around his cock, testing the thickness. It was rock hard with a silky skin, and she was intrigued by his masculinity. "Does this feel good?" she asked, slowly stroking her fist over his erection.

"You have no idea."

Lori smiled, excited that she was able to affect him with a simple touch. It gave her a sense of power, and she savored the fact he wanted her just as much. "You have no tattoos. I thought bad boys always had some."

"My body's my own. Nobody gets to brand me." There was such emotion in those few words, and she wondered what he'd been through when he was younger. He'd told her horrible bits and pieces, and she was sure the full picture would shock her to the core. All they could do now was start over, make today the first day of forever.

"I love your body," she said. Lori reached up and held his shoulders. "You're so strong. So hard."

He grit his teeth, then grabbed her waist, hoisting her up on the wooden kitchen table. "Lean back on your elbows," he said.

She did as instructed, carefully resting back on the table, her entire body never so exposed. He squeezed her thighs, staring down at her with the eyes of a predator, a man hanging desperately on the edge. Chains leaned over and kissed her stomach, making her giggle. He kept kissing up her center, higher and higher until he reached her breasts. She clenched her pussy, swearing the wetness would leak down to her ass.

Lori gasped when he covered her areola with his mouth. He supported her tit with one hand, his tongue painting patterns around her nipple. She closed her eyes and dropped her head back as he suckled her, the pressure in her womb building and building.

"I want you to remember today," he said. "I want you to remember when I made you mine."

She loved the sound of ownership in his voice. Lori wanted to belong to Chains. He was the first person to make her want to live.

He shifted lower, slinging both her legs over his strong shoulders. "What are you doing?"

Chains gave her a wink, then disappeared between her legs. When his tongue swiped up her folds, she squealed. He growled as he spread her pussy lips apart. He thoroughly explored every inch of her, his tongue flicking her clit before penetrating her deep in her cunt.

"Chains … oh God." She spiraled out of control, the overload of sensation making her feel more animal than woman. She thrashed beneath him, but his strength was unsurpassed. His rough stubble scraped her inner thighs. He held her steady, eating her pussy until she was panting and begging him for release.

Just when she thought she'd have the orgasm of the century, he pulled away, standing tall. He stared down at her, still positioned between her legs.

"I'm going to enjoy taking your virginity, baby. Open for me." She didn't hesitate, bracing her heels on the edge of the table, wanting his mouth on her clit again.

He licked his finger, then slid it inside her pussy. She clenched around his digit, wanting his big cock instead.

"Fuck me," she said.

"Such a dirty mouth for such a pretty girl." He tutted, dragging that finger down to her ass before impaling her nether hole. "This will be mine, too."

He kept his finger in her asshole, wiggling it in such a way that she swore she saw stars. The explosion of sensation made her clit throb in distracting waves.

"Stop teasing me." She barely managed to get the words out, so lost in her own wanton desires.

"Let me play, sweetheart. Trust me, it'll be better this way." He removed his finger, then scooped her naked body up into the cradle of his arms.

"What are you doing?"

"I'm not fucking you on the table. Not for the first time, anyway." He carried her to his room. The curtains were drawn, so it was a bit difficult to see. Her sense of smell was magnified, and the room reminded her of Chains—deep, intoxicating, musky cologne, leather, and control.

Lori had always scraped by in life, her nerves always on edge. She wasn't good at survival, but she'd done it every day. After being beat up by Carlton Riggs, struggling to make ends meet at her shitty job, and terrified of the future, she saw Chains's arrival as a godsend. His confidence in every situation put her worries at ease. He made her feel protected, cared for, and wanted. He was her addiction.

He set her on the edge of the bed, and she wiggled up to the center. Chains stood at the end of the bed, one arm across his chest as he grabbed his shoulder.

"Sure you want to give yourself to me, Lori? Where I'm from, I'm considered garbage, the lowest of society. You deserve more, but I'm a selfish bastard."

She narrowed her eyes. If anyone had lowly roots, it was her. Her parents were on government assistance, living in one of the worst ghetto areas of the city. She didn't care about the past, just now. "You talk too much." Lori reached down between her legs and touched her sensitive clit.

He shook his head. "Hell no, that's *my* job, baby."

Chains crawled up onto the bed, with the stealth and intensity of a predator. Every muscle flexed as he closed in on her. Her heart raced, her body reacting to his proximity. He used his thigh to spread her legs open, then hooked his arms under her shoulders, holding her close. His hard cock pressed against her pussy, making her wetter. A mix of excitement and apprehension of what was to come had her entire body hotwired to his touch.

She expected something fast and forgettable for her first time. Chains took his time, once again proving he was more than just any man. He kissed her, deeply, passionately. His kisses felt like promises, and she savored every one of them. The entire world and its problems went away, leaving just the two of them in this little piece of paradise.

Lori ran her hands over his shaved head, then held his shoulders as they kissed.

"This is perfect," he said. "You and me … it feels right." Lori couldn't agree more. She leaned up and kissed him again, loving how easily she could pull him back under the spell. His cock twitched, and those kisses soon moved down her neck. "I love these tits," he said before squeezing her cleavage together. He played a game with his tongue over her nipples that had her toes curling.

"I want you inside me," she said. "Please."

"You don't have to beg. That's exactly what I'm planning." He reached between them, taking hold of his big cock. As soon as he rubbed the thick head long her moist slit, she sighed in relief. She needed him more than breath. "I'm going to go easy at first. You let me know if I hurt you."

She nodded, her nails digging into his biceps as her anticipation grew stronger. He pressed the tip inside her, joining them, even if only an inch. She used her muscles to squeeze around him, getting used to the foreign invasion. Chains cursed.

"More."

He took a deep breath, ever so slowly pushing more inches inside her. She'd been so wet and ready that he had no trouble sliding home. Once he was fully seated, he ran his lips along her jawline and didn't move his body. She felt so full, so completely stuffed with his cock. Her virginity was gone—given to her captor, her lover.

"You're mine now," he whispered. Her eyes lolled back in her head as he shelled her ear with his tongue. "No other man will know this body but me."

Forever sounded perfect to her. She craved security, commitment, and the happily ever after she'd never expected for herself. Her goal had been to give her siblings a better chance than she'd had. She'd given up hope for herself so many years ago. Now everything was new again.

"Don't leave me," she said. The words were pure vulnerability, her deepest fear vocalized.

"Never, sweet girl. We were meant for each other. I knew that from the first moment I saw you." He pulled his cock most of the way out, then filled her up again. "I never thought I'd fall in love. The whole idea was a joke to me … until you."

"I love you," she said. Yes, it had been less than two weeks, but she didn't care. It was the truth, a soul-deep confession that had to be said.

****

Chains had been waiting for this day. He was balls deep inside the only woman who'd managed to get under his skin. Her pussy was hot and tight, squeezing him like a fist. And she'd only been his. She had no idea how valuable he considered the gift of her virginity. Having been born with nothing, he knew Lori was his prize.

After taking her from the diner, he'd worried she'd hate him for kidnapping her, even if he believed it was for her own good. A one-sided relationship would never work. To hear her express her love for him was more valuable than all the money in the world, and he'd never make her regret falling for him.

He was done waiting. Chains began to fuck her, working her slow and steady, building up a good rhythm. Her little mewling sounds proved she wasn't in any discomfort. It didn't take long for her to arch up to meet him thrust for thrust. Her pussy was drenched, and he could already feel her spasming around his cock.

Chains kissed her lips. "Your body was made for fucking," he said. All her soft, lush curves were heaven. Her juicy tits jiggled beneath him, and those thick thighs spurred him on. He'd never get enough of his woman.

The more he fell for her, the more terrified he became. He had something to exploit, something an enemy could use against him. Not smart for a hitman. But he was beyond turning back now. And he wasn't the first man at Killer of Kings to get serious with a woman. Lori had just become number one in his life.

"Do you like my dick inside you, baby?" She nodded, her lips parted as she fought for breath. Her eyes were glazed over, but he demanded an answer. "Say it. Tell me what you want."

"I want your big dick. I want it deep inside me,"

she said.

Damn, he loved hearing her talk dirty. He had so many filthy plans for her this week.

His muscles felt invigorated, and he swore his entire body could go all night long. Lori did that to him, brought out his beast.

Chains reached between them, circling her clit with his thumb as he continued to pump into her cunt. As he supported himself up with one arm, the angle gave him the perfect view of Lori as her orgasm crested. The little sounds she made only made him harder.

"So good…" She moaned and writhed on the bed, her hands grabbing at the blankets.

"Come for me, sweetheart. Just relax and let go." Within minutes, she detonated, her pussy clamping down on his cock. "It's okay, I've got you."

He dropped over her, letting her ride out her orgasm. Watching the passion in her eyes, knowing he'd bound them together, was enough to make him come. He filled her with his seed, pumping his hips until he was completely spent.

*You're mine now.*

Chains rolled over to the side, deep satisfaction washing through him. He needed that. And now that Lori had lost her virginity, he didn't have to worry about hurting her next time. He was already envisioning the many things he wanted to do with her.

"Thank you," he said.

She shifted to her side, facing him. "That's a funny thing to say."

"You gave him something special. You have no idea," he said. "The women I've fucked around with were nothing I'd want for more than a night."

"And me?"

"You're my princess." He cupped her face,

running his thumb along her lower lip. "And you've just changed my entire life."

Lori had to come number one, even before Killer of Kings. He hoped it never came to choosing sides because he respected Boss, enjoyed his job, and wanted it all. He'd been in contact with Shadow recently during a job, and the other killer seemed to succeed in mixing business and pleasure. Around the same time, they'd met El Diablo, even getting along … until now. The bastard never should have broken into his house. A man's home should be off limits.

"How long do we have to stay here?" she asked.

"Just until things cool off. And I obviously need to get a better security system at home. El Diablo managed to bypass it way too easily."

"But he's a professional killer, like you, right?"

"Maybe, but we're not on the same side. Not yet, anyway." His mission was supposed to be recruiting the renowned hitman for Killer of Kings. Boss had a plan to lure Xavier in, but all Chains wanted right now was alone time with Lori. "It'll all be dealt with soon. Nothing to worry about."

"At least he didn't try to kill me. I know you're mad at him for breaking in and everything, but I really believe he thought he was doing a good thing by setting me free."

Maybe the ruthless killer had a bit of humanity left in him after all. Chains didn't want to dwell on it. He'd already been thinking too much about that crazy bastard.

"He's lucky he didn't hurt you, because then I'd have to hurt him. Well, kill him. After torturing him."

The look on Lori's face reminded him he needed to keep some of his life on the down low. Lori was sweet innocence, and he didn't want her completely tainted by his world. Or scared. "I don't want anything to happen to you, Chains."

"Nothing will happen to me. I know how to survive. I'm not new to any of this. That's why Boss recruited me long ago."

"When you came to this country?"

"From Russia. Whatever shithole you're used to, my neighborhood would make it look like Beverly Hills."

She touched his face. At first, he flinched, not used to allowing a woman to get so close. "I can't hear much of an accent," she said.

"It's there, but only when I want it to be. I know a lot of languages. It comes with the territory."

"You must have some happy memories as a child. Is there anything you can remember?" She sounded genuinely concerned, and it touched his heart. Lori was a good woman, and he'd never let her go.

"I had friends in the orphanages, but after the things I witnessed happen to them, I learned to keep my emotions in check. If you don't have emotions, you can't get hurt. Know what I mean?"

She smiled warmly. "I understand. But, if you don't let anyone in, you can never know love."

"I know love," he said. Chains was still reluctant to make any declarations to Lori. Things were still in limbo, and he didn't want to risk his heart just yet. But he knew what he felt for her, and it terrified him. He needed to change the topic. "What about you? What's a happy memory you have?"

"I have a lot," she said. "Seeing the happiness on my little sister's face when I bought her a grade eight graduation dress. Or paying for my brother's school trip to the zoo. He was so excited."

"Those are all other people's happiness," he said.

"That's what makes me happy."

Chains was pissed off. Those were all things a parent should be worrying about. Lori struggled like a dog to provide happy memories for her siblings. He'd change all that. He wasn't sure how, but he'd make sure her brothers and sisters were taken care of so she could enjoy her own damn life.

"You're too good for me, baby." Chains pulled her closer, tucking her into the crook of his arm. "I don't deserve you."

"Don't say that," she said. "I've never been happier. I don't know what I'd do without you now."

He loved hearing her say those words. Chains wanted her to need him, because he'd be working hard to make her dreams come true. He'd never been responsible for anyone but himself, and it felt empowering to have another life to care for.

They cuddled together until they fell asleep. Chains wasn't sure how much time passed, but his pager vibrating in the kitchen woke him up. He checked on Lori, and she was still sound asleep. Carefully slipping off the bed, he tugged on a pair of shorts, and closed the bedroom door behind him.

He checked his pager. It was Maurice, so he called him back on his cellphone.

"What's up?" he asked.

"Your cell was off."

"Yeah, well, I'm laying low right now. Since that piece of shit got past my security system, I needed to get off the grid."

"Since when have you been afraid of a fight?" asked Maurice. "I thought you were Boss's go-to man."

Did he know about Lori? As far as Chains knew, she was his dirty little secret. "I'm just playing it safe. You have a problem with that?"

He heard Maurice sigh on the other end. "El Diablo took the next bait. That means he's on target for interception in two days."

"Boss know?"

"Of course Boss knows. This is part of his plan. He'll be there with Killian. He'll expect you to be there, too. El Diablo trusted you the most. You did spend a lot of time with him."

"That doesn't mean we're best friends. I don't know shit about him. And a man like El Diablo doesn't know anything about loyalty."

"Boss doesn't see it the same way. Anyway, this was a courtesy call," said Maurice.

"For what exactly?"

"Boss knows about your plaything. He doesn't like secrets."

## Chapter Nine

Lori rolled over and moaned. Her body felt so incredibly sore, and it wasn't in a bad way either. Recalling the way Chains had taken her, it made her all warm inside. Opening her eyes, she reached out only to find the bed cold. Frowning, she glanced over at his side of the bed, and he wasn't there.

She sat up and glanced around the room, and hated that he wasn't there. For a long time when she was home with her family, she craved sitting at home all alone, just to have a few moments to herself.

Right now, she felt lonely. She hated feeling that. Tucking her hair behind her ears, she tried to listen for any sign of him. Chains wouldn't abandon her here.

Pushing the sheets off her, she made her way through to the bedroom. Dealing with her morning routine, she decided to take a quick bath. While the water ran, she stared at her reflection in the mirror, surprised by how different she looked. She didn't recognize herself. Pursing her lips, she wondered if she felt any differently.

She didn't look away from her curves like she once did. Instead, she turned this way and that, seeing her red breasts from Chains's loving, and also the bruises from his touch on her hips. Her lips even felt a little swollen from his kisses.

Once the bath was full, she tested the temperature. She'd already put in some bubbles, so she climbed into the tub, easing back, and closing her eyes, basking in the joy of being in the water. The warmth eased some of the soreness. It was nice to just relax.

Seconds passed, maybe even minutes, before she felt him.

Opening her eyes, she saw him completely dressed, arms folded, leaning against the doorframe. Heat filled her cheeks as she remembered the passion he'd shown her last night.

"Morning," she said.

"How are you feeling today?" he asked.

"I'm okay."

He moved toward the toilet, and she didn't like how pensive he seemed to look. Not that she could read Chains very well. He always kept to himself, and she was no mind reader.

"You're not sore?"

"Why weren't you in bed?" she asked instead.

"Are you sore?"

She glared at him. "I'm fine. Why weren't you in bed?" When he made to speak she interrupted him. "I answered two of your questions. The least you can do is answer one of mine. It's the nice and polite thing to do."

"You gave me your virginity last night."

"I remember. I was there."

"Yeah, and now it's the morning."

"So?" She stared at him hoping that he'd give her something other than the blank stare. "What is all this about, Chains?"

"Women have a tendency to make decisions they regret."

"So do men."

He chuckled. "Losing your virginity is not as big a deal for men as it is for women."

She rolled her eyes. "You think I'm going to regret what we shared together?"

"There's a chance. I wouldn't be upset with you if you did."

"Wow." She really didn't know what to say about that. It made her wonder if he'd been in situations where women had regretted being with him. "Have you been hurt a lot?"

"Women don't hurt me."

She took a deep breath. "I don't regret what we did. I hated waking up alone. That was … upsetting."

"Why?"

"I had sex for the first time with a guy who decided to take me off the street. The one chance I had to leave and I didn't want to. I've felt you inside me. I want it again, and the morning after, you're not there. Was I not good?"

"You were perfect."

"You see, Chains. This can go both ways. For all I know you hated what we shared."

He moved closer, kneeling on the floor beside the bath. "I didn't hate it. I loved every single second of being within you. For as long as I live I will never forget how you felt when I claimed your pussy, or the way you cried out with pleasure when I made you come. Even the tightness of your ass around my fingers."

"That was kind of kinky."

"I'll make you beg again and again for me. You'll never want for anything. That I promise you."

"I do like your promises." She took his hand, lifting it off the edge of the tub, and kissing his fingers. "I like being in your arms."

"I … you're the first woman I don't want to hurt, Lori."

She smiled. "You couldn't hurt me." She pressed his palm against her cheek. "I love being with you."

"I was wondering how you'd feel about staying here for a few weeks. I've got to leave tomorrow to take care of some business. When I get back, I want to spend some time, just you and me."

"You're going to leave me here?"

"You'll be protected. And I won't be long. This is our safe house."

"Can't I come with you?"

"I don't want you to be hurt. Please, do this for me."

He looked so stressed out that she relented. She didn't want him to be worried about her. "Fine, but it will cost you."

Chains sighed. "What will it cost me?"

"Share this bath with me?"

He glanced down at the water then at her. "You want me to share the water with you?"

"Yes. Come on, Chains. I've got you for one day. Consider this my payment. I expect you to do everything I want for the entire day. Twenty-four hours, do you think you can handle that?"

He rested his forehead on the side of the tub. "This is a hard decision."

She giggled. "You're teasing, aren't you? Oh my, my stone-cold killer is joking around. I like that."

"I am not."

"I bet you don't even know how to tell a joke." She saw his eyes crinkle as he smiled, and that look on his face was a dream to see.

She couldn't resist touching his face, staring into his eyes. This man, he was a total mystery. He confused her all the time, and especially the feelings he inspired in her.

There's no way she could ever walk away from him.

She'd do whatever he wanted to put that smile on his face.

Leaning forward, she pressed her lips against his, and smiled. "So how about that bath?"

"You want a day of being in complete control then I'm happy to be at your mercy. That means you stay here. You don't leave this house until I return."

"Yes, and when you get back, I will be here waiting, and hoping that we can have some fun." She winked at him. "Does that make you feel better?"

"Yes."

She didn't know why he was so determined for her to stay at home, but she wouldn't argue with him. Chains clearly had a reason for doing everything.

He stood away from the bath, and she watched him undress.

Lori kept her gaze on him, feeling herself heat up at the sight of him. Biting her lip, she pressed her thighs together as he revealed himself to her. His cock was long and thick, and already leaking pre-cum. There wasn't an inch of fat on his body, just hard-cut muscle.

Chains stepped toward the tub and urged her forward. She didn't argue with him as he sat behind her. With a hand over her stomach, he pulled her back so that she rested against his chest. Closing her eyes, she placed her hands on top of his thighs, and basked in the closeness of him. He felt so amazing to her, so warm, so right.

He pressed a kiss to her neck. "What else will my lady be demanding today?"

She chuckled. "That's for me to know and for you to find out." She liked this, being close to him, having him completely at her mercy.

"I don't suppose I can do this?" He stroked his hands up her stomach to cup her tits.

Lori gasped. "That's more than fine."

He pinched her nipples, and she arched up wanting more of his touch. "Damn, that is a pretty sight, watching how much you want me to touch you."

"I don't want you to stop."

"Lift your legs and place them either side of the tub."

She looked up at him, confused.

"Do as I ask?"

"This is my day, remember? I'm the one that gives the instructions."

"And I will follow them, baby, but will you ask me to play with your pussy or would you like me to take the lead on this, and to play with you?"

In response, she lifted her legs, placing them over the tub.

"Good girl."

One of his hands moved from her breast sliding down her body. When he touched her pussy, she cried out. Any soreness or discomfort disappeared as he began to run his finger between her slit. He stroked over her clit, pinching the nub before moving down, plunging a finger deep inside her.

"You're so incredibly tight, and I know it's because my dick is the only one you've ever had. That makes me so fucking hot, Lori. You're all mine. Every single part of you." He nibbled on her neck, and the pleasure pulsed through her entire body.

He pulled his finger from her pussy, drawing it back up to her clit, and stroking her. The hand on her tit pinched her nipple, tugging on the flesh. She felt her arousal increase, and she wanted his dick inside her.

"Fuck me, Chains," she said, begging him. She didn't want to go another second without him inside her.

"You want my hard cock sliding in your pussy?"

"Yes."

"Then turn around."

She pulled her legs into the tub, which was large enough for her to spin around.

"Wrap your legs around me, and take my cock in your hand, put me inside you."

Lori followed his instructions, not caring that she

was shaking just a little. She was so aroused and desperate for his cock.

He was already so hard that pressing him against her pussy wasn't difficult. Inch by thick inch he sank into her wet heat, and she squeezed his shoulder where she held on for dear life.

"Now that is sexy as fuck. Seeing you take my cock, feeling your tight cunt wrapped around my dick." His hands moved to her hips. "Now start to ride me, baby."

She held onto both of his shoulders, and slowly, she took him deep inside her, pulling up until only the tip of him remained within her.

Finding a slow pace, she quickly got accustomed to his thickness, and it wasn't long before she was driving herself down onto him, wanting more and more.

"That feels so fucking good."

He moved from her hips to grab her ass, speeding up the tempo. He drove up inside her, over and over. She cried out his name, the pleasure building inside her. One of his fingers trailed between the crack of her ass, teasing her anus as he fucked her.

"Touch yourself, Lori. Touch your pussy. Make yourself come on my cock."

She fingered her slit, thrusting up and down on his length. Her orgasm began to build, and it shocked her with the force of it as she came hard, driving down onto his cock. She screamed his name, their pleasured sounds echoing off the walls as he made her come at the same time his growl joined hers and his cock kicked within her.

Lori felt every single pulse as he filled her pussy.

Pressing her face against his neck, she tried to calm down her rioting emotions, but they were all over the place. Over and over she took deep breaths, basking in his touch as he slid his hands over her body.

"You feel amazing, Lori. I'm the luckiest bastard alive to have you."

She felt like the luckiest woman in the world, and she didn't want to lose him.

****

Chains shook his head. "I'm not doing that."

"Yes, you are. This is still my day. I've fed you breakfast, and we've watched a horror flick, which I think was a bad idea. I hate horror films."

"Why did you watch it then?"

"Because I knew you wanted to watch it, and because of that, I figured I'd do something for you for a change." She swung her hips from side to side, clapping her hands in time to the beat of the music.

Since his conversation with Maurice the night before, Chains had felt tense. He didn't doubt that Boss knew about Lori. The son of a bitch probably had every single little detail on her life and was basking in his downfall. Another Killer of Kings to be lured in by the pleasure of a woman.

Lori was … fire to him. She was like a drug he didn't want to give in to. All of his life he'd given everything back to people or had it taken from him. He didn't want to give her back. She was a treasure. No one else cared about her. He did.

She came back to him, and that meant fucking loads to him. There's no way anyone was ever going to take her from him. He'd kill every single one of those bastards first.

He wanted Lori to stay here while he went and dealt with El Diablo and Boss. If he didn't think Boss would be a problem, he'd take her with him, but he knew Boss, and that man would find some way for him to pay.

There was a reason Boss was the leader of the

Killer of Kings. No one got anything past him. He had more kills than any of them. In fact, his list of skills, kills, and deals was so long that some people believed they were mere speculation. He'd heard Boss's name whispered as being in cahoots with the devil himself.

Chains just figured there was a lot more to Boss than any of them would ever realize. Boss always made the decisions. He kept to the guidelines, and he never crossed the line unless he had to. He was fearless.

"Where did you go?" Lori asked, standing in front of him. Music played in the background.

"It's nothing."

"You can tell me whatever is on your mind," she said.

There were some things that would absolutely terrify her. Boss was not for the faint of heart.

"You want me to dance with you?"

"Yes." She smiled at him. Getting up from his seat, he moved toward the stereo and changed her bubbly pop music for something heavy, filled with rock. She groaned, and he swung his head, making the movements as if he had a guitar in his hands.

"Now this is what I want to dance to." He took her hand and pulled her against him.

"You can't dance to this noise."

He laughed, gripping her hips. "You'd be surprised what you can dance to. Feel the beat, baby." He held her close so that her ass nestled against his cock. "You feel that?"

"Your erection?"

"Well, feel how hard I am, but also feel what I do to you." Back and forth, he guided her in a dance. Her body melted against his, and she didn't fight him either.

When the song changed to one of her bubbly pop songs, she pulled out of his hands, threw her arms up in the air and began to dance. "Come on, Chains, you've got to learn to adapt. To change, and to be part of it all. Whoo." She jumped from side to side, and deciding to throw caution to the wind, he gave in, and started to dance with her.

She bent forward and laughed so hard as he swung his hands in circles, and started to do some pecking thing with his head.

"Oh my God, that is so funny." She spun around, and together they danced crazily. The song lasted for three and a half agonizing minutes, but when it turned into a slow ballad, Lori was instantly in his arms.

He held the base of her back while also keeping hold of her hand.

Staring into her eyes, he was completely blown away by the feelings that she inspired inside him, and it wasn't sex either. He didn't want to think about what those feelings meant right now.

"I like dancing. I could never do it at home. There wasn't a lot of room, and no one liked listening to music. I know it's silly."

"I loved doing it. You've got nothing to worry about. I hope we do this more often." He closed his eyes, hating her family once again. If he ever met them, he was going to murder them. Maybe Boss would do it for him and then he wouldn't have to worry about her being upset with him.

See there was a benefit to having him around.

"I really enjoy being with you, Chains. Like this. I..."

"What is it, Lori?"

"I ..."

"You don't have to be afraid." He was worried now.

"I don't want you to leave me. I'm not a needy

woman, and I don't want you to think that I'm begging or anything, but I really like you."

He slammed his lips down on hers, silencing her words. Hearing the desperation in her voice, it tore at him. Sliding his tongue into her mouth, he breathed her in. She wrapped her arms around his neck, and he held her tightly.

"I'm not going to leave you. I'm going to do whatever I can to make sure we're always together."

"I know your work is dangerous, but I won't ever get in the way. I'll be by your side."

When he'd taken Lori, he didn't have any expectations. He'd seen her, and unlike normal guys who'd have asked for her number, he decided to take her instead. No one was perfect, and he was aware of his faults.

The music turned, and it was back to rock music.

Letting her go, he began to rock his head, with the guitar back in his hands, and when he stared at Lori, he saw she was doing the exact same thing.

He'd never allowed himself the pleasure of goofing around, and that was how Lori wanted to spend her day. After a couple of hours of laughing and joking, they collapsed on the sofa. She took his hand, and held it tightly.

"Where you're going tomorrow, will it be dangerous?"

"Yes and no. I've got to get two people to meet. It's not going to be too dangerous, but the guy that saved you, he's wanted."

"Like a criminal?"

"My boss wants him. It's not going to be a big deal. You don't have to worry about a thing."

"When you get back, you'll teach me how to fight? How to stop someone like El Diablo from hurting me."

"I'll teach you everything you need to know." She snuggled in against him, and he played with a lock of her hair.

"Do you go abroad?" she asked.

"You're asking a lot of questions tonight?"

"I'm just curious. Dancing with you, knowing where you've come from. I want to know everything about you."

"Tell me something about yourself?" he asked, avoiding the question.

She shook her head. "I'm a completely boring person, Chains. You know that. I'm one daughter of many children. I spent a great deal of time taking care of my brothers and sisters while trying to make sure they got an education. I went out to work, fed us all, clothed us. It's not a very colorful life story. Unless you count suddenly being taken late one night after taking out the trash."

He chuckled.

"Then my life got really exciting. I was chained to a basement, fed amazing food, held at gunpoint. Being forced to leave my kidnapper only to come back. See, kind of boring."

"I don't know, your kidnapper sounds awesome. I bet they were top of the range chains."

She burst out laughing. "See, you're full of surprises. You told a joke. It was a very funny joke."

He kissed her head.

Yes, he'd told a joke. He wondered if this was one of the reasons Boss didn't like his men falling in love with women. He didn't feel any softer, but there was a time he'd have shot someone before telling a joke.

Lori was special though, and he wanted her to see him differently than just a killer. To her, he wanted to be a man worthy of taking her virginity. It meant a great deal to him.

# Chapter Ten

He left before she woke up. She'd only worry, and he didn't want any emotional distractions—not today. Lori would be safe at the cabin, and he'd find out where he stood with Boss before he returned to her. He couldn't punish him for having a woman, not when he gave his blessing to at least four other hitmen on his payroll. As far as he knew, being committed to a woman didn't affect their performance on the job. Same would ring true for him—he'd prove it if he had to.

Once he hit the main highway, his GPS said he'd be at his destination in just over an hour. He turned on the satellite radio, and cranked the music. Yes, he hated Xavier for breaking into his house, but Boss had planted a file there. It had been part of his plan. Maybe Chains was more disappointed in himself than angry at Xavier. He really didn't expect that bastard to jump through all Boss's hoops successfully. And he never thought Lori was in danger. The security system had been activated, and Chains had only been gone a few hours. He needed to be smarter.

He zoned out as he drove, his mind going in several directions. El Diablo was more like him than he cared to realize—both forced to survive with the odds against them, both sadistic enough that Boss wanted to recruit them. Chains remembered when he first met Boss. He swore he'd met the devil himself. The owner of Killer of Kings was in his home town on a contract hit with a couple of men. One of them was Viper.

Chains had worked his way up the ladder, working for a powerful Bratva doing hits and shakedowns. He was able to maim and kill with no remorse, a sought-after quality in his line of work. From an early age, he'd gone numb in the emotions department, a safety mechanism thanks to his shit childhood.

Boss had been there to kill the man he worked for, the kingpin of the organization. Chains was young, but he still managed to put up one hell of a fight. That was as far as he got, but instead of making an example of him, Boss ended up offering him a position at Killer of Kings.

It hadn't take Boss long to uncover every detail of his miserable life—crooked orphanages, unspeakable abuse, and a life of crime and violence. But he saw deeper, saw Chains's skills and the person underneath all the bullshit. He had pity on him.

*"What's with the scars?" Boss asked.*

*They were on a plane to America, Chains leaving everything behind. Boss had the seat beside him at the front of the plane—the very best money could buy. Chains rubbed his wrist, looking down at one of the permanent reminders he wanted wiped from memory. "Chains."*

*Boss nodded. "You survived. That's what counts," he said. "Bottle that shit up and use it to your advantage."*

They never spoke more about his sins or any of the horrors he'd endured. Boss probably knew it all anyway. Now he saw something in El Diablo.

Once he neared his location, Chains sat straighter, more on alert. They were meeting at a shipping yard, mountains of colored containers creating a maze of metal.

He dialed Killian. "You on site?"

"Just pulling in. Keep on the down low. El Diablo will be going for the yellow office trailer near the dock."

"It looks like business as usual around here. Boss prepared for the collateral damage?"

"We're professionals, eh?"

He hung up and drove around back. His trunk had everything he'd need if things got ugly, but the whole point of this venture was to blackmail Xavier into a job at Killer of Kings. Even if things went down without a hitch, which was unlikely, he still had to explain himself to Boss. He hadn't lied, just failed to offer every detail of his life. Lori was his business, no one else's.

His custom holsters were full, his jacket hiding all the heat. He parked and walked around the area. The place was bustling—trucks backing up, cranes loading containers, and every sort of bell and whistle. With all the dock workers, there would be a bloodbath if Xavier decided he wanted nothing to do with Boss's offer. He patrolled up and down the aisles between stacks of metal containers. Everything had gone too smoothly. El Diablo was either a genius or a fool for making it to the end of Boss's trail of breadcrumbs.

He didn't have a good feeling about any of this. It wasn't Boss's style. His instincts were screaming at him to get out.

If Xavier was indeed like him, then he was smarter than this.

Chains walked to the edge of the dock, looking down at the water lapping the sides. He'd left a cell phone with Lori for emergencies, and he called it to ease his mind.

"Took you long enough."

His blood turned to ice, his muscles tensing. He kept still, the horn from a boat sounding off.

"Nothing personal, Chains. But, if I were you, I'd make sure you play nice." Of all his men, Boss had to send Bain. He was a sadistic bastard.

"If you touch her—"

"Relax. She doesn't even know I'm here," said

Bain.

He paced back and forth. "I don't get it. What point does Boss want to make?"

"Keeping a woman hostage in your basement is kind of fucked up, no?"

"Does she look like a prisoner?"

Bain exhaled. "Look, I couldn't give a shit, but your extracurricular activities are making you sloppy. Did you put on false plates when you drove Boss to that poker game the other day? You think company vehicles aren't tracked?"

He paused. Fuck, he'd been so worried about leaving Lori alone in the basement that he'd been making stupid mistakes. He'd used the same car to drive Lori to the damn cottage. So much for his hidden retreat.

"We weren't tailed."

Bain scoffed. "You willing to bet her life on it? Having a woman in our line of work complicates everything. Makes you a liability. You have to be on top of your game every second." The line went silent. "According to Boss, you'll have unwanted visitors within the hour."

"I'll leave now."

"You leave, Boss gives me the go ahead to torch this Popsicle stand."

Another test.

Boss wanted him to be one hundred percent loyal to Killer of Kings. The man had a hard-on for control. If Chains sacrificed the mission or Boss's safety, Lori's life could be in danger. If he stayed, her life was in jeopardy as those mobsters looked for revenge. He couldn't win this.

"You wouldn't dare," he said. "Do you know who the fuck I am?"

Bain laughed. "You know exactly what I'm

capable of, so don't test me. Boss said to break her legs first. That's if she survives the fire."

"You're a real piece of shit," he said. "I'll stay. Don't go near her." Then he added. "She's all I have, Bain. If anything happens to her … I know where you live." He hung up the phone.

No problem. Get El Diablo to sign on with Boss, then race back to the cottage before anyone could get there. He took a deep breath, knowing this entire mess was due to his inability to separate business and pleasure. All these emotions were new for him. He was used to going in headlong, not caring about consequences or worrying about getting hurt. Boss kept him close because he had nothing to lose and everything to gain. Things were different now.

Thanks to Lori he cared more about survival. She was his salvation. Or would he lose her, destined to always end up with the short stick in life?

At this point, he didn't care about appearances. He pulled out a Glock, holding it just inside the lapel of his leather jacket. His heart still raced, a powerful sense of betrayal making him see red. How could Boss do this to him after so many years of loyalty? Chains was a fool to think that monster could actually care about anyone but himself.

He found the trailer and didn't bother hiding until Xavier showed up. He opened the door and barged inside. There were two men sitting having coffee.

"Break time's over. Get out." Usually his size and appearance were enough to get results without having to get physical. When they didn't move, he repeated himself in Russian. Then they scurried out with no argument.

Chains sat down on the swivelling chair of the main desk, lifting up both legs to get comfortable. What was so damn important that El Diablo would go on this goose chase? The final file should be here, in this specific trailer. Chains pulled open the top drawer and saw an envelope marked "Top Secret". He grabbed it out and tore off the seal. He wanted to know exactly what the fuck was going on around here. He slid out the paperwork and examined it.

*Interesting.*

Boss was skilled at finding the slightest weakness to use against a person, and it appeared that even the Colombian devil had an Achilles' heel.

He waited, leaning back in the chair, wishing he could be heading back to the cottage. Anyone who hurt his woman would suffer severely. It wasn't much longer when he heard the handle rattle. He pulled out his gun and aimed it at the doorway, his arm crossed over his chest as he palmed a second.

The moment El Diablo's head popped into the trailer, he had instant recognition. They'd spent quite a bit of time together last time Boss had him tail the hitman. He'd do just about anything for money or pussy, and it surprised him he had this sensitive spot to exploit. It was probably why he had had pity on Lori.

He released the handle of the second gun, still aiming the first, then wagged the envelope in the air. Xavier immediately slipped inside, slamming the door shut behind him.

"That's not for you, big boy. Hand it over."

Chains smiled. "I've already read it."

Xavier licked his lips, his dark eyes unreadable. "What do you want?"

"All I care about right now is my woman."

He nodded. "Oh, I get it. This is about that girl I set free from your makeshift prison. You're a real piece of work, buddy."

Chains sat up straight, bringing his legs down. "Listen, it's not what you think. She came back to me. I'm going to marry that woman."

"I think both of you need some counseling."

"I have something you want, but you're not getting it so easily," said Chains.

"I can shoot you right now and take it."

He smirked. "I'd love to see you try." He opened his jacket, revealing his one-man arsenal.

"Tell me what you want."

"The reason you're here. The reason this exists." He shook the file in the air. "It's all because Boss wants you working for Killer of Kings. Consider this his recruitment."

"Do I have a choice?"

"You can choose to walk out the door, but you don't get the information, and Boss won't be all too happy."

"And that's it?"

Chains exhaled. How much should he tell this fucker? He cared enough to release Lori in the first place, and after reading the paperwork, he knew the devil had a heart. "Boss won't let me leave until you agree to sign on. I need to leave."

"Hot date?" Xavier winked.

"Someone I pissed off is heading to my cottage right now, looking for revenge. Considering my woman's there alone, I'm real motivated to get this shit moving along."

"She locked in the basement again?"

"Fuck off, Xavier."

"El Diablo to you," he said. "I have nothing to do. How about we take a ride, and then I'll come talk to your Boss."

"Don't play games with me. You're going to

work for Killer of Kings?"

"I've seen your place, so I know they pay well. What can it hurt, right? Consider our road trip a way to put water under the bridge."

"Okay, let's do this."

****

Lori woke up and showered. She didn't expect Chains to be in her bed. And she needed to get used to him coming and going without constantly worrying about him. He was all she had now, and the way he made her feel … she couldn't lose that.

After having a light breakfast, she noticed an SUV parked down the road, partly shrouded by brush. Had it always been there? Chains's car wasn't in the driveway.

He said they were at his cottage because it was too dangerous at his home right now. She was safe. The man who'd released her was supposed to be a madman, and the threat of him returning was enough to make Chains pack up and leave his house.

She glanced over at the kitchen table, looking for the cellphone Chains had left her. It wasn't there. She wandered around the cottage, checking the counters and ledges, even inside drawers. Where had she put it? Great, if something happened she had no contact to the outside world. She took a deep breath, calming herself. He said he wouldn't take too long, so she could wait. This was a little piece of paradise, so who was she to complain?

Lori put on her jacket and shoes, stepping out onto the wraparound porch. The view was spectacular, one side thick forest and the other looking down onto a valley. The air smelled of pine and black earth, a welcoming contrast to the stench of the city where she grew up.

She'd never been one to exercise, too busy

working, then too tired to care. Maybe she'd take up hiking. Lori ventured down the steps, running her fingertips along the wild flowers. She felt so free, so happy. Chains had turned her entire world around. It may have started off a little unorthodox, but she couldn't complain now.

Lori picked up a good-sized walking stick and used it as she entered the forest. It was a different world under the forest canopy. The birds sang, and squirrels scampered in the branches above her. She could hear the faint sound of a creek in the distance, so she kept going, hiking deeper and deeper into the forest.

She wasn't sure how much time passed, too enamored by the beauty of the nature around her. Lori had never had time for fairy tales, but right now she felt like she was in the middle of one. She'd lived such a sheltered life, so much still to learn and explore. When she heard branches cracking far behind her, her nerves picked up. She looked back and saw nothing, but realized she'd hiked far enough that she'd have trouble finding the cottage again.

Should she be more afraid of wild animals or El Diablo? She crouched down behind some briars, peeking down the beaten path again. A swath of fabric made her breath catch. Was she seeing things?

Then she saw him. Lori would recognize that face anywhere. His dark hair was pushed mostly off his face, his black eyes focused. Chains was right, he'd come looking for her. This time she had a feeling he wouldn't be so generous.

A sudden wave of dizziness left her head swimming. There was nowhere to go, and even her cellphone had vanished. When he kept coming closer, no longer trying to hide, she decided to take her chances. She got up and started running. The branches and twigs of the unbeaten paths scratched at her exposed skin, but she couldn't slow down now.

"Hey, stop!"

*Yeah, like that's going to happen.* Lori wanted to live. She needed to survive until Chains came home. Her mind was a mess. Where would they be safe? Would life with him always be like this?

When she stopped to take a breath, peering behind her, she noticed two men coming from another direction. What the hell? She'd never seen them before. Had Chains sent them to protect her? Were they hunters? She decided anyone was better than El Diablo. A stitch in her side slowed her up, but she moved in the direction of the strangers. She braced the trees as she roughed it through the overgrown paths.

"Lori, stop running!" El Diablo was catching up on her. Damn, she was out of shape.

The other men started to come into better view. They looked like they belonged in a night club, not the middle of the wilderness. That's when she noticed they had handguns, and once they got a clear view of her, one of them aimed and fired. She screamed and ducked down, not knowing which way to run. So much for her carefree romp in the forest. The only thing she could do was venture deeper, away from all these murderers.

Another bullet whizzed by her head. She was too hyped up on adrenaline to cry or scream. Her focus was survival.

The next time she turned to gauge their distance, she saw the violent spray of blood come out the left side of the lead man's head. He collapsed heavily to the forest floor. The other guy briefly looked down at him before continuing the pace, right toward her.

*What's happening?*

Lori had been so transfixed on the nightmare in

front of her that she hadn't focused on El Diablo coming from her other side. He bent down and grabbed her, hoisting her effortlessly to her feet. She used all her strength to kick and punch him, struggling like a wild woman, but he wrapped a solid arm around her body, pinning her arms to her sides.

"Relax."

"Let me go!"

The other man was getting closer. Were they together? Would they torture her? Kill her? When El Diablo's chest rumbled in laughter, she thought he'd lost his mind.

Then she saw him.

Chains.

He came up behind the other man, wrapping an arm around his neck, and knocking the gun out of his hand. It disappeared in the leaf litter. "I thought we made ourselves clear, motherfucker. The city is Killer of Kings' turf, and now you've just crossed the line."

The man gurgled, his face turning red.

"You shot at my woman." Chains let him go, shoving him to his knees. "Grab your gun. I fucking dare you."

The guy got to his feet, and Chains punched him in the face, once, twice, and a third time. They started going at each other, kicking, punching, and shoving with skills she'd only seen in the movies. As the other man stumbled back, he reached for the gun, but before he could aim, a bullet when right through his hand. He screamed and hugged his arm, blood leaking down.

Lori gasped.

"Nothing to worry about," said El Diablo. "Your boyfriend's got this handled."

She remembered when he'd murdered Carlton for hurting her. He was a killer. And he was hers. Chains grabbed a gun from his shoulder holster and put a bullet in the man's head, right between the eyes as if he'd done it a thousand times—maybe he had.

He started coming for her, and instead of feeling afraid or sobered, she only felt relief. A shadow appeared from behind a tree on the path Chains had taken. A third man? He didn't have time to turn all the way around when a bullet stopped him in his tracks. Chains crashed sidelong against a large oak, pointing his gun despite his injury.

Chains didn't need to fire back, because the third man dropped to the ground. They all stared, everyone frozen and silent, not daring to move a muscle. Where was the other gunman? Who would be shot next?

El Diablo used one arm to hold her, getting his free hand onto a handgun.

"I told you it was nothing personal." A huge man dressed in black came out into the open, his arms covered in ink. "But weren't you supposed to deliver the package to Boss at the docks?"

"Would you take a chance with Scarlett's life, Bain?" asked Chains.

"Yeah. Guess I wouldn't."

"At least my cabin's still standing. I was expecting a pile of ash."

"Nice piece of land you have here."

Bain pulled out his cellphone and turned around as he talked to someone. She could only make out a few words like "handled" and "three of them".

She struggled in El Diablo's grasp, and he released her. Lori rushed over to Chains, throwing herself in his arms. Even his scent brought down her nerves. He winced.

"You're shot," she said. Lori wanted to examine him, but he only held her close to his chest. He kissed the top of her head.

"I'm okay. What about you? Did anyone hurt you?" he asked.

She shook her head.

"I'm so sorry, baby. All I could think about was getting back to you."

Bain put away his phone. "Boss is waiting to see the three of you. I wouldn't keep him waiting too long. I'll be meeting Viper in the city to make an example of whoever sent these bastards. Boss's orders. They don't know what's coming."

The way he said the words made her shudder. Whoever he was after was not going to have a good day.

## Chapter Eleven

He took a cleansing breath once they were alone in his cabin. Bain agreed to give them a little alone time before heading back to the city. Lori wrapped her arms around his waist, resting her head on his chest. "I was so scared. I can't lose you."

"Everything's okay now." He stroked her hair and kissed her atop the head.

"Your heart's racing. You're lying."

He pulled away, shaking his head. "Boss won't hurt you. Killian won't let him."

"But you think he'll hurt *you*? I thought things were settled."

"He's going to want to punish me."

"Punish?"

He didn't like the fear in her eyes. His job was to protect her from the dark side of his life. "You know about my Boss. You know what I do for a living. My life's complicated, and not in a good way. Maybe you're better off without me." She was his prize, but now he loved her enough to let her go. He wouldn't let Boss hurt her. That crazy bastard had shot other women without remorse. He was capable of anything.

"Don't say that."

"It's true. I'll set you up so you never have to work again, never have to worry."

She pounded on his chest. "Stop it!" Her eyes glistened with unshed tears. "I'm not going anywhere without you. We're together in this. Do you understand me?"

"I made a big mistake. Let me fix this. Be smart, Lori."

Tears streamed down her face. "No! I love you. I won't live without you."

Fuck, she was cute when she was angry. He cupped her face and kissed her hard on the mouth. He needed her, had to be as close as possible. Chains backed her up against the wall and tugged her shirt off over her head. "I need you," he said.

"I won't let you leave me, Chains. Never suggest it again."

"Yes, ma'am." He unfastened her bra and bent down to gorge himself on her tits. He was addicted to her body. She mewled as he toyed with her nipples. They both needed this, needed to blow off some steam. Needed to forget reality for a while. He stripped off her pants and undies until she stood completely naked. "Put your leg over my shoulder."

When she didn't comply, he helped her, tossing her leg over his shoulder to give him a nice view of her pussy from where he knelt. "Chains…"

"Don't deny me, Lori. You're my little piece of paradise right now." He lapped up her folds, making her cry out. He closed his eyes and rubbed his face against her cunt. She was already wet, her clit throbbing when he latched on. Chains suckled her until her leg went weak.

"I can't take it anymore."

He dropped her leg and stood up, towering over her. Chains shrugged off his jacket, forgetting he had his gun holsters on. But they clearly didn't scare Lori, and she ran her fingertips along them, her lips parted as she looked up at him. He could feel her wanton energy, and it only increased his tenfold.

"I want all of you, princess. You ready to give me everything?"

She nodded.

Chains removed his holsters and unbuckled his pants. All that mattered was right here, right now. His cock was rock hard, tenting out his boxer briefs once he kicked off his pants. "Tonight's a good night to break in the kitchen table," he said. "Lean over it for me, will you, baby?"

He watched her walk to the table, her beautiful body naked, all her curves jiggling in just the right way. They maintained eye contact, even once she'd passed him. God, she was beautiful. In such a short time she'd transformed from an insecure, shattered woman to a strong, confident one.

She did as told, leaning over the wooden slab table on her forearms, her lush ass waiting for him. He licked his lips, reaching for the lube in the drawer near the sofa. With everything so up in the air, his need to claim every inch of his woman overwhelmed him.

"Remember when I told you this would be mine one day?" He rubbed a circle over the globe of her ass. "Today's that day."

"I trust you," she said, no hesitation in her voice. He repeated the words in his head. Chains was used to being considered a heartless monster, a cold-blooded killer, not a man worthy of a woman's trust. He would never let her down because he considered her love and trust a gift.

He kissed her ass, smoothing his hand up her back, pressing her down. Chains poured the lube down her crack, then used his finger to rub it into her tight little rosette.

"That feels good."

"Such a cute little asshole. Tell me you're mine."

"I'm all yours, Chains."

He inserted one finger into her virgin hole, moving it in just the right way to make her crave more.

\*\*\*\*

Lori squeezed around Chains's finger. She never realized how good something so dirty could feel. He'd set off something inside that affected her whole body. She needed him, all of him.

He ran the broad head of his cock up and down the crack of her ass, distributing the lube. Each pass made her clit and ass throb. She wasn't sure if he was toying with her or preparing her.

"Chains, please…"

"This is different. It'll feel strange at first." He gripped her hip with one hand and pressed the head of his dick into her ass with the other. "Push back against me. Once I'm in things will get easier. Promise."

Yes, he'd kidnapped her, kept her against her will, but that was then, before she knew the real him. She trusted Chains completely, knowing he'd never do anything to intentionally harm her. The first few inches made Lori cringe—the pressure, tightness, and unfamiliar sensations nearly made her change her mind. But Chains was right. As soon as the full length of his big cock was deep inside her ass, she became accustomed to the intrusion.

He stayed in place for the longest time, running his fingertips up and down her back, playing with her hair. She could stay like this forever.

"You should see what I see, baby. My cock inside your tight little ass. You feel amazing."

She tightened around him, making him groan. Lying on the cold, hard table, her bare breasts pressed flat, she was completely vulnerable. New, dirty thoughts flitted in her head. Her beast of a man had claimed her ass, claimed all of her, and she loved every minute of it.

"How do you feel?" he asked.

"Better."

"I'll go nice and slow. You let me know if I hurt you."

She nodded, using one hand to grip the edge of

the table. He slid out, then pushed back in, slowly picking up a steady rhythm. In, out, in, out … it didn't take long for her to be transported to that beautiful place of pre-orgasmic bliss.

"Oh God, Chains. I'm so close already." These new sensations were powerful and exciting. She had a feeling this would be an orgasm to remember. Her entire body heated, her cheeks flushing.

He grabbed her wrist, bringing her arm down alongside her. "Touch yourself." He brought her hand between her legs. "Make yourself come while I fuck you."

As soon as she touched her throbbing clit, she gasped. Chains picked up the pace, pounding into her ass so hard the table legs scraped the tiles. His big, rough hands squeezed her hips as he rammed her.

"Chains!"

"Come for me, Lori." His voice had taken on a darker edge, a man barely holding onto his humanity. It turned her on to see him so caught up in their lovemaking. Just hearing his command was enough to push her to the breaking point. Her womb cramped, then detonated, a beautiful rush of heat and pleasure rippling through her body.

She felt him ejaculate inside her ass as he pumped a few final times. They were both breathing heavily, their bodies moist with clean sweat. He pulled out and held a hand to her back. "Wait here a second."

Chains came back a few minutes later and wiped a warm, moist cloth over her intimate parts and inner thighs, tenderly cleansing her.

"Thank you for that," he said. He beckoned her to stand, taking her hand until she was standing in front of him. He arranged her hair, tucking the remainder behind her ears. "God, you're beautiful, Lori." Then he gave her a single kiss on the lips. It was the most precious moment of her life, so much emotion and promise in that one act.

"Now what?"

"We face the music," he said.

She shook her head, taking a step back. "I can't risk him hurting you."

"What do you suggest, baby? There are no options."

Lori tossed her hands in the air. "We run away. I mean, what if he decides you deserve a death sentence? I say forget everything and we go, no looking back."

"He'll find me."

"No, he won't! We'll live off the grid. Live happily ever after." Tears clouded her vision.

Chains pulled her into his strong arms, his heat and masculine scent surrounding her. She focused on the steady beat of his heart, trying not to break down completely.

"We'll get through this. Please don't cry," he said.

They got dressed, tension strong in the air. Once she was ready, she stood frozen in place as Chains rushed around, checking his weapons. Everything seemed to be happening in a daze, a dreamlike state. She couldn't even imagine losing the love of her life.

"Lori!" Chains held both her shoulders, giving her a little jolt. "Listen to me, understand?" She nodded. "I have money. A lot of fucking money. I put all the information in my bottom dresser drawer. If anything happens, take it all. Pay for all your brothers and sisters to get a good college education, buy yourself a cute house far from here. Understand?"

Her mouth opened, but no words came out.

## Chapter Twelve

Chains kept on kissing his woman. He didn't want to let her out of his sight for a moment. Sitting in Bain's car as they headed toward wherever Boss was living didn't fill him with confidence. He wrapped his arm around Lori, pulling her in close. She settled against him, and he loved the way she just melted next to him as if she didn't want to be anywhere else but at his side.

El Diablo chuckled, breaking the silence. "Any sane woman would be thankful for my help, but not this one. She went right on back to the loser that was keeping her captive."

Lori tensed up, and Chains glared at Xavier.

"It wasn't like that," Lori said.

Chains kissed her head again, tucking her in close. It was exactly like that, but he'd given her a much better life than the one she'd been living.

"Yeah, because you're suffering with Stockholm Syndrome or some shit," El Diablo said.

"You're a sick fuck," Bain said.

"That better be directed at me." Chains wouldn't have any of them bad mouthing his woman. He was the one with the issues here, not her.

"Let's keep this going. So, when did you two meet?" El Diablo asked.

"He came into the diner where I worked."

"And how did you end up in his basement? I admit that it was a pretty nice basement, but still. Chains certainly likes to give his prisoners the best."

Chains closed his eyes. He didn't want nor did he need to hear this shit right now. "Are you done?"

"Seriously, Chains, what did you do?" Bain asked.

Glancing down, he saw Lori smiling up at him.

"It is kind of weird how we met, isn't it?"

"Do you regret it?"

"No, not for a single second."

"He has her completely brainwashed." El Diablo put a finger against his head, and gave it a turn.

"He's never hurt me, or done anything that makes me fear for my safety." He saw the smile in her eyes, the love shining back at him. This was his fucking prize for all those years of torture and abuse. "He's taken care of me."

"See, I'm telling you, cuckoo."

"Shut the fuck up," Chains said. "If I didn't have to deal with you I wouldn't be heading to see Boss. He's probably got a huge stick up his ass over this."

Bain snorted. "He'll get over it."

"You're telling me he didn't sound pissed?" asked Chains.

"Oh, he sounded pissed. He wasn't happy with what you did with Lori. That's really put you on his shit list. All things considered, that's an achievement. I don't know if I should be proud of you or fucking afraid for you," Bain said.

This didn't bode well for him at all.

Boss demanded excellence. Not only had Chains taken a woman against her will, he'd also been completely sloppy at work. Boss didn't mind a lot of things, and in fact, he often looked the other way, but sloppy work didn't slide.

Running a hand down his face, Chains squeezed Lori's thigh. Whatever happened, he would do what he could to protect her. He loved her more than anything else in the world.

She was his woman, and his very reason for living.

"You look worried," she said.

El Diablo snorted. "He should be pissing himself with fear."

"Shut the fuck up," Chains said. "I don't need a lecture on shit from you when you don't even know what you're dealing with." He stared down at his woman. "It'll be okay."

"Why do I feel like you're lying to me?"

"Because he is," Bain said.

"Enough, you two. Stay out of my fucking business."

"It's your business why I'm here, Chains. I could be with Scarlett right now, enjoying another long vacation, but as it is I'm dealing with this bullshit. Tell me why I would help you out or even stay out of your business?" Bain glanced at him in the rear-view mirror. "Did you even fucking think about the consequences of your actions? She could have family that went out hunting for her. Do you really think Boss would have handled a shitstorm that long or that involved? Killer of Kings is a secret organization, and you can't just snatch people off the streets because you feel like it."

He heard the anger in Bain's voice.

The man was right.

If Lori had been anyone else, if her parents had given a shit about her, this would have ended a lot differently. It hadn't though, and he wasn't worried, not even a little.

"Did my parents try to look for me?" Lori asked.

"What?" This came from Bain.

Chains glanced over at El Diablo and saw the man looked uncomfortable, no humor on his face.

"You heard me," Lori said. "You mentioned my parents. Did they go to look for me? Alert the cops? Anything?"

"It doesn't matter," Bain said, looking tense.

"You're the one to bring it up. I'm a big girl. I can handle myself, and I know the answer anyway."

"Then you don't need me to say it."

"I want to hear you say it."

Chains didn't know what his woman was getting at, but he remained quiet.

"Did my parents try to find me at any point? Even put out a missing persons report?"

"No." Bain's voice was muffled as if he was speaking through gritted teeth.

"I didn't hear that."

"No, there was no missing persons report or even a notice that you hadn't been home."

"It was like I just left one day, and they didn't even care," Lori said. She shrugged. "I don't think you should be using my parents as an example. They didn't even notice a daughter gone."

She rested her head on Chains's shoulder. Placing a finger beneath her chin, he tilted her head back.

"You okay, baby?" he asked.

She nodded. "There's no point being sad about that. I knew my parents didn't care about me."

"Do you want me to kill them for you?"

"You'd do that, wouldn't you?"

"In a heartbeat."

"No. I don't want that. They don't matter any more to me. All that matters right now is you, me, and that I've got to some way get you out of trouble with your boss."

"His name is Boss."

"So you've got a boss named Boss?"

"Yes."

"And people think I'm weird. That is just a little more weird."

Whatever Boss wanted to say to him, he'd handle

it.

He'd been handling everything all of his life. There hadn't been anything worth fighting for then, but with Lori, she was worth everything.

"You're really ready to take on Killer of Kings?" Chains asked El Diablo, changing the conversation. She didn't need to know that when they met Boss, it could end really badly for him. Their outcome depended on Boss's mood.

"May as well now that he has me by the balls. Pay sounds better, and there's a lot more benefits."

"The work is harder, more challenging. Boss demands total loyalty," Chains said. "Whatever you wanted to be before, or whoever you were taking targets for, they will cease to matter."

"The world is full of bad men. It'll be interesting to see what you guys do. You all keep going back to him, so he must have golden balls or something," El Diablo said.

Chains chuckled, and rested his head back. When he met Boss, he'd been a shell. His skills rivaled all, but he'd been dead inside. There hadn't been much there until Boss brought him back, and gave him focus, and a reason to kill.

Now that he had Lori in his arms, everything seemed complete to him.

"I wouldn't have hurt her," Bain said, speaking up.

"What?"

"Lori, I wouldn't have hurt her. Boss gave me a few simple instructions, but none of them were to kill her. As a matter of fact, he wanted me there to protect her from those hitmen. He's not as bad as you think."

"You told me you were going to torch my house, and to start breaking bones."

"I told you what I'd been told to say. Boss said that I was to take her to him, and that he'd deal with you there."

Lori took hold of his hand, squeezing it tightly. He didn't want to let her go, not now, not ever.

"Are we going to die?" Lori said.

"No, we're not."

Chains was more determined than ever before to make sure Boss listened to him. He'd been loyal to the man and to Killer of Kings. Every single job he'd been assigned, he'd completed. All of him, every part of him, had been all about the company. There's no way he was going to give up the one thing that made him human.

Boss had helped to make him a man, a human killing machine.

Lori was the one who made him better; she made him feel.

El Diablo raised a brow when he looked at her.

"You can't guarantee that shit." He spoke in a way not to alert Lori.

Chains smirked.

These two men had been near his woman a handful of minutes and already they didn't want to hurt her feelings or scare her. She had that aura that drew men, making them want to protect her.

It also helped that her own family had cast her aside.

Killer of Kings were men with dark pasts. Their histories were what nightmares were made of.

Lori had a past.

She'd been forgotten, and the men felt guilty for highlighting that.

The drive toward Boss took way too long. The sway of the car made him sleepy. It had been a long couple of days. All he wanted to do was curl up with Lori in his arms and go to sleep. There would be time for that soon enough. For now, he had to protect Lori with his very life.

**** 

Chains had lied to her, but that was okay. Lori knew he was doing it to protect her, not that she needed all that much protection. Whatever happened, she was going to take the few weeks she'd been with Chains with her. They were the best weeks of her life, and that meant a lot to her.

She never thought that she'd fall in love, or that happiness would ever be within her grasp.

The car was pulled into a hotel parking lot, which did surprise her.

"A hotel?"

"This is a Killer of Kings hotel, Lori. This is where we make bad shit happen and can clean it up without anyone noticing."

This made her shake. Chains didn't let her hand go as they climbed out of the car. Bain stood by her side and El Diablo next to Chains. They headed toward the main doors where men with guns were waiting.

This didn't bode well for either of them. Biting her lip, she tried to keep the fear locked inside, but again, that wasn't helping.

The men looked at them with that horrible smirk that she'd come to associate with all of their colleagues. Chains held onto her shoulders as they entered the elevator. She smiled at him in their reflection of the mirrored box. If he was there with her, she knew she'd be safe.

Placing her hands on top of his, she saw him smile back. When they first met, Chains's smile was … scary. He didn't really know how to do it, and he always looked so sad. That was changing, and she was pleased to have been part of it.

"I love it when you smile," she said.

"You're the one I smile for, baby, all the time." He pressed a kiss to her temple, and she closed her eyes, loving his touch. She'd gladly stay in his arms all day long.

"I love you, Chains, so much."

His arms moved from her shoulders to around her body.

"I was thinking about our wedding," he said.

She smiled, liking this conversation. "Am I in a white dress?"

"Absolutely. I wouldn't expect anything less."

She saw Chains had surprised his friends.

"Would we get married in Vegas?"

"No. It would be a small wedding. Something modest. A couple of witnesses. We'd have a big cake, and I mean a huge one."

"I like that idea."

"Me too. I love cake. You'd have to work on your vows."

"Would you write your own?" she asked.

"Of course. I'd say how much I love you and that I would work to keep you safe, and never hurt you, not ever."

She leaned back against him. The elevator was taking such a long time.

"That sounds so beautiful."

"Do I get an invitation to this wedding?" El Diablo asked.

"I don't know. If Boss doesn't shoot your ass, we'll see."

The elevator doors opened, and she felt Chains tense behind her. He tried to hide it, but she always felt a difference in his body, and right now, every part of her was screaming to protect, to keep him safe. It was probably weird considering he was the one with the experience in weapons.

No one had ever tried to save her man, and she wanted to be the first. She wanted to prove to him that she did love him, and it wasn't about some stupid kidnapping thing. This was the real deal.

Yes, he'd taken her.

In the beginning she'd been scared of him. Who wouldn't be? She'd woken up in a house she didn't know with a strange man. Her love for him hadn't been instant. It had taken her time to see that he was just lonely, and broken like her.

They stepped off the elevator, and turned a corner.

Down a long corridor, she saw a door. It was made of glass. Everything seemed to be made of glass.

Chains took her hand, and she squeezed him, trying to offer him comfort.

Entering the office, she saw a man sitting behind a desk. He was staring straight ahead at them, his gaze on Chains before moving to Bain then to Diablo. Finally, his gaze was on her, and she knew without a doubt this man was Boss. The one they all feared and that was easy to see why.

There was darkness in his eyes and nothing else.

He didn't speak. No one spoke. The air grew tense, and Boss just sat there.

There seemed to be a standoff going on, and Lori didn't know what to do so she stood a little in front of Chains, hoping to direct the other man's rage away from her man.

"Did you get the file?" Boss asked.

His voice was clipped, straight to the point, and demanding respect.

"Yes. El Diablo is now officially a Killer of Kings employee. Congratulations," Chains said.

Bain stepped away, holding out the paperwork to Boss.

He didn't take it.

Another scary looking man with a twisted lip took the file from him, opening it up. "He did it. El Diablo now belongs to you."

"Hold on one fucking second," El Diablo said. "I don't belong to anyone. Not now, not ever."

"That's not what was agreed. You're still your own person, but your ass belongs to me and Killer of Kings," Boss said. He turned to Diablo. "The information I got for you didn't come cheap. I know you think you're the fucking devil, and you can do what you want, but that ends. You're not going to best me, so don't even think of trying. Do you understand me?"

He waggled a finger in the air. "I don't know who the fuck you—"

Before El Diablo could finish, Boss had taken a gun and shot him in the forearm he'd outstretched.

Lori gasped, holding onto Chains even harder.

"Oh fuck!" El Diablo cradled his arm, pain clear on his face. Blood dripped down to the tiles.

"Now, that hasn't entered a major artery. Nothing's broken. You're good at what you do, I will grant you that, but you're nowhere near the best. I demand the best, and that is exactly what you'll give me, do you understand?"

She saw the inner battle in El Diablo, but the man finally nodded.

"Good, I like having you on the team." Boss's henchman held his hand out, and El Diablo looked more like he wanted to stab the man than take his hand. "Don't be a fucking pussy. We've got plenty of nurses that will be more than happy to patch you up. If you want to use them for more, do so. I don't care, but get the fuck out of my office right now."

El Diablo wasn't offered any more assistance. He left the office without a backwards glance.

"Did you think that was smart?" Bain asked. "He's a deadly motherfucker."

"He's all bark and no bite. He'll get the work done that I need." Boss's gaze finally turned to Chains, and then his gaze was on her. "Now, I have to deal with another problem." The gun he held in his hand was directed at the both of them. Boss kept changing the person he pointed at. "Now what do I do with this problem right here? Because this *is* a problem."

"It's not," Chains said.

"You kidnapped a woman off the street, took her to your basement, and now you think you're going to live happy fucking after?"

"Yes, I did all those things."

"You nearly ruined the reputation of Killer of Kings, Chains. Do you know that? You nearly fucked with what I have. I don't like that." Boss held his gun out steady, and Lori gasped, putting herself in front of Chains.

"No, don't kill him."

"You need your bitch to fight your battles for you as well now, Chains? You're not man enough to take me on by yourself?"

She shook her head. "No. Please stop. You've got this all wrong. I love him. I love Chains. Yes, our beginning was a bit weird, but who cares? He loves me, too, and we're going to be together. We're going to get married. I'm not going to say anything about what you do. Please, don't kill him." She felt her tears suddenly building, and before she could stop them they were streaming down. "I don't want to live without him. He's been the only one that has ever cared about me, and I don't want to lose that. He means everything." The moment she started talking, the reality of losing him was just too great. She couldn't handle that, nor did she want to. All of her life she'd been pushed aside, unloved, unwanted.

Chains was the only one to see her, to care about her, to love her, and she couldn't let anything happen to him. She wouldn't be able to survive it.

With tears blurring her vision, she stared at the man that she knew could end her happiness with a single shot from his gun.

Staring into death's eyes, she placed herself in front of Chains. "Please, I'm begging you, don't kill him. I couldn't … I don't…" Words were failing her. She only felt this overwhelming sense of grief.

"It's fine," Chains said. His hand banded around her. He tried to move her out of the way, but she refused to budge. Not this time. She wasn't going to let him be taken from her. She couldn't.

Licking her dry lips, she kept her focus on Boss. He looked bored, as if this was all a little tedious to him.

"Kill me instead." The words left her mouth, but the moment she said them, she knew she'd surprised him.

Was that a good thing?

## Chapter Thirteen

"Out of the room." Boss pointed to the door. "I need to speak with Chains alone."

"Are you going to hurt him?" asked Lori.

Boss didn't look ready to humor her.

"It's okay, baby. Just business. I'll be out soon," said Chains.

Lori looked back at him as she left the room, the door finally clicking shut behind her. He hated being caught in this position, but he could only blame himself. When he'd taken Lori from behind the diner, it had been pure instinct. There was just something about her that called to him, demanded he keep her as his reward for a fucked-up life. He hadn't used a level head then or when he went on his last assignment with Boss. Chains knew firsthand what happened to hitmen who left loose ends or turned sloppy. Boss demanded perfection. He was obsessed with keeping the reputation of Killer of Kings hard as nails.

"So…"

"I know I fucked up, but it won't happen again," said Chains.

Boss tapped a pen on the desk, swiveling slightly back and forth in his chair. "Of all people, I wouldn't expect you to take a prisoner. I mean, fuck, after the shit you've been through it doesn't make sense."

"She wasn't my prisoner. Not for long, anyway. We both feel the same way about each other, so I don't see a problem."

"Of course you don't. But I guarantee you'll cost me money and the lives of my men if you keep screwing around on the job. I can't have it. I *won't* have it."

He wanted to ask what was next, but kept his mouth shut. Why was Boss stalling? Just put a bullet in his head and get it over with. Once Boss made up his mind, nothing he could say would change a thing regardless.

"I keep you close for a reason. I trust you, and you always give me your best. When I need a driver, intel, guaranteed hit, anything … I call you and get results."

"That doesn't have to change."

Boss stood up and rolled out his shoulders. "Viper and Bain are off to clean up your mess right now. Even though you fucked me over, I won't tolerate anyone trying to take out my men. The only thing going for you is getting El Diablo to sign on with Killer of Kings."

"Because you blackmailed him."

Boss shook his head. "I got information he couldn't. Nothing's free, Chains. Not in this fucking life." He walked back and forth in front of the hotel windows, admiring the skyline.

Apparently when El Diablo was sold off to a gang as a child, he hadn't been the only one. He had a younger sister, but she'd disappeared when he tried to find her as an adult. Boss managed to find her, but he required loyalty in exchange for the information.

"Lori's innocent. I got her mixed up in this shit, so please leave her out of this. I know I screwed up, but I gave you a lot of good years. Surely that counts for something." It was his last request, one more chance to try to ensure Lori didn't get hurt.

Boss nodded slowly as if lost in thought. "I have to make an example of you, Chains. Whether I want to or not."

"What does that mean?"

"I've always loved that property of yours up north," said Boss. "And you really believed I didn't know about it? Cute."

Killian sat on the edge of the desk, looking bored.

"Let's not bullshit around. What have you decided?" asked Chains.

Boss smirked, walking around with his hands clasped behind his back. "You remind me of Killian. I brought you both to America, both orphans, both used to living in shitholes. Everything went great until you found women."

"Then why am I the one being punished?"

Boss tutted. "You want to know what I decided? Tell him, Killian."

Killian ran a hand through his blond hair. "You said you were going to fire him."

"Fire him," Boss repeated. "That's never happened, has it, Chains?"

He shook his head.

"Of course not, because I don't fire people, I make them disappear. No potential problems that way."

"I'll go far away. I won't make any problems for you or the company, you know that," said Chains.

Boss laughed, an evil, twisted sound. "You'd love that wouldn't you?" Then he stopped in his tracks. "Like I've told you before, I can't leave you unpunished, and that wouldn't be punishment. So, you'll be in charge of training El Diablo. That whiny bastard will be your shadow until he meets Killer of Kings' standards. After that point, you can choose to walk away or stay on. As long as there are no more fuckups."

"Fuck that shit. I can't stand that pompous asshole. I won't do it!"

Lori burst back in the office, rushing over to him. "Chains! Take the damn deal," said Lori.

Boss and Killian chuckled. "Better listen to your woman, Chains. She's a smart one," said Killian.

She looked up at Chains, pleading with her eyes, holding him tighter. Some of the tension in his muscles eased.

"Fine." He said nothing more.

"Thank you," she said to Boss.

"I didn't do it for you, sweetheart." He turned to Chains. "I did it for him. He's always been like a son to me."

Boss jutted his head to Killian, and the other man reluctantly got off the desk. He clapped Chains hard on the shoulder before walking to the door. "Better you than me, eh?" Killian laughed as he left.

"El Diablo will be healing up for a while. He's a real fucking pussy. Take the next couple weeks to get your shit together. And take care of your girl. She's been through enough." Then he pointed to the exit.

Chains rushed them out to the elevator once given the chance. "I can't believe he pulled this on me."

"How are you complaining? I thought I could lose you, Chains."

"Training recruits doesn't take a couple weeks. This isn't a department store. It'll take years. That means years of dealing with that prick, having him underfoot constantly."

"He's not so bad. He set me free, remember?"

He growled after a lengthy silence. "I'm an idiot."

"Why would you say that?"

"I worried about me instead of thinking about you. You're absolutely fucking right, baby. We're both alive, and we have each other. That's what matters."

They held hands. "I don't ask for much. I just need you," she said.

"Since I'm alive and well, which is better than I expected, we'll still be paying for your brothers and sisters to get a good education and on their feet. You love them, and whatever's important to you is important to me."

"Thank you."

"Remember when I asked you to tell me your happy memories. And they weren't about you?" She nodded. "I understand now. Because I've fallen in love."

They kissed slowly, sensually.

"Good and bad, I'm here. I'm yours," she said.

"I'd go through all the bullshit in my life all over again if I knew you were the prize." He cupped the side of her face, using his thumb to wipe away a tear.

"I love you, Chains. I'd still be in the same miserable place in my life if you hadn't come in my diner that night."

He winked. "You were right about the pie." They both smiled, remembering the crazy memories. "And I promise I'll spend the rest of my life treating you with the love and respect you deserve."

She collapsed against him, and he held her tight. Together, they headed back to the cottage. Their little slice of heaven. She'd never look back, never regret a thing. She may have come from lowly roots, but Chains made her feel like a princess.

They'd saved each other, both given a second chance at happiness. Chains may be a killer, a hitman for hire, but he was hers, and she wouldn't change a thing about him.

The End

www.samcrescent.com

www.staceyespino.com

EVERNIGHT PUBLISHING ®

www.evernightpublishing.com